DELTA DEPUTY

Center Point
Large Print

Also by L. P. Holmes and available from
Center Point Large Print:

Singing Wires

DELTA DEPUTY

L. P. HOLMES

CENTER POINT LARGE PRINT
THORNDIKE, MAINE

This Center Point Large Print edition
is published in the year 2024 by arrangement with
Golden West Inc.

First US edition: Doubleday and Company, Inc.

The text of this Large Print edition is unabridged.
In other aspects, this book may vary
from the original edition.
Printed in the United States of America
on permanent paper sourced using
environmentally responsible foresting methods.
Set in 16-point Times New Roman type.

ISBN: 979-8-89164-339-0

The Library of Congress has cataloged this record
under Library of Congress Control Number: 2024940981

CONTENTS

DELTA DEPUTY

I—Spanish Slough

Rolling just fast enough to keep ahead of the dust which churning wheels sucked up, the stage jolted its way along the narrow levee road to the western approach of the Spanish Slough ferry. Here the road broke sharply from the levee crest to the ferry landing below, and the battered old Concord went down this short steep slope with skidding rear wheels and the dry squeal of straining brake blocks. Pulling to a stop, the stage driver stood up, whipped himself with his arms against morning's dank chill, cupped his hands about his mouth, and let out a pealing yell.

Over at the far bank of the slough the ferry barge tugged sluggishly at the bridle which looped up to the overhead guide cable. Over there also, set half on earth and half on crusted, sodden piling, was old Joe Imbaugh's weather-beaten shanty, its rusty chimney filtering a thread of pale driftwood smoke into the air.

The driver's hail brought a growling shout in answer, and then Imbaugh and his burly half-breed assistant came out of the shanty, threw off the mooring lines of the barge, and went to work on the windlass. The grease-blackened guide cable sagged and swayed, the pull line whined thinly on the windlass drum, and the barge moved slowly and ponderously into the crossing.

Inside the stage, Dan Scoville stirred his rangy length and laid another brief, wondering glance on his two fellow passengers. Both were so immersed in some problem of their own they neither returned Scoville's scrutiny nor seemed aware of it. It had been that way, all through the morning's ride.

The man was a gangling sort, faded of hair and eye, with a narrow face which reflected a strained but obstinate stubbornness. The woman showed the same faded drabness as her man. Gaunt and weary in figure and spirit, beaten by time and hardship to a colorless neutrality. The kind of people, reflected Dan Scoville, that life had a way of rolling over and leaving behind in the gray dust of failure and hopeless frustration.

His restlessness growing, Scoville opened the door of the stage, climbed out, and stamped his boot heels against the earth to quicken circulation gone a little numb from chill and inactivity.

Far out to the east, so distant and lofty as to seem little more than cloud masses, the soaring crests of the Sierra Nevada Mountains were limned against morning's quickening glow. But here all about and close to the earth, there was nothing but a pale, cold mist which was night's lingering breath, given off by the sprawling width of this vast delta land.

The stage driver grinned down at Dan Scoville. "What's the matter with Bid Hazen and his missis—they too paralyzed to move?"

Scoville shrugged. "Wouldn't know. I'm not throwing rocks at either you or your stage, understand—but I've known more comfortable rides."

The driver whipped his chilled arms again and cackled a thin laugh. "You bought transportation, friend—and that's all you were guaranteed. As for Bid Hazen, mebbe it ain't the ride that's got him stiffened. It could be something else."

Having no idea what the driver was hinting at, and not being particularly concerned, Dan Scoville dug a pipe from the pocket of his corduroy coat, packed it, ran a flickering match across the bowl, and savored the smoke's fragrance keenly as he moved out ahead of the stage and watched the slow approach of the ferry barge with deep-set, reserved, and bleakly cool blue eyes.

Under the level set of his hat and against the turned-up collar of his coat, his face showed lean and brown, a little taciturn. There was a direct intensity to his glance and a faint hint of pressure at his lip ends which suggested that here was a man in whom a certain capacity for violence lay couched at all times, but it was a violence which he could control or turn loose in a degree to fit the demands of the occasion. His legs were slightly bowed, telling of plenty of saddle work. His flanks were narrow, and he had a wiry torso which tapered up into a pair of good, solid shoulders. Now, as he maneuvered the worst of the stiffness from his muscles, he moved with a certain soft, sure ease.

The ferry barge nudged the bank, and the half-breed was swift with the mooring ropes. The approach apron slammed down, and Joe Imbaugh waved a hand to the stage driver.

"All set, Sage!"

The stage team of four came ahead gingerly, snorting a little, hoofs ringing hollow on the timbers of the barge. The stage lurched after them, and the barge creaked and settled under the weight. The driver, an old hand at this business, judging distance and space with exactitude, set his brake again. Dan Scoville stepped aboard, and the half-breed pulled in the mooring ropes. Joe Imbaugh, turning to the windlass again, looked up at the stage driver, then tossed a short nod toward Scoville.

"Hauling light today, eh, Sage? Only the one?"

"Three," corrected the driver. "Bid Hazen and his missis are inside."

The beginning creak of the windlass stilled as the grizzled ferryman straightened and turned. "No! Is Hazen crazy?"

"Or mule stubborn," declared the driver. "Mebbe both. Anyhow, it's his pie and he can slice it any way he wants."

Joe Imbaugh considered this for a moment, then shook his head and bent again to his windlass. The ferry edged slowly out across pale brown water which sucked and gurgled. From some hidden pothole beyond the slough a wild mallard quacked greeting to the new day. Upstream, a bank of tules disgorged a cloud of blackbirds, and their passage was a sibilant rushing in the air as they winged off to some distant feeding ground.

Over past Joe Imbaugh's shanty, where the road began again along another levee top, dust spiraled thinly up and then two riders hove into view, dropped from clear outlines into the morning shadows below, cut around a corner of the shanty, and stopped at the ferry's eastern approach. The half-breed, facing that way from his end of the windlass, grunted something to Joe Imbaugh, who turned, had his look, then swore softly.

"Cole Logan must have had a hunch. That's Duff Twining and Waco Dart. They wouldn't be here just for the ride. Now if Bid Hazen is lucky, he'll face nothing worse than a long walk back. But if his luck's run out, then—!" Imbaugh finished with a shrug.

The stage driver had marked the arrival of the two riders, also. He dropped his glance to Imbaugh, and spoke carefully. "You know, Joe, I'm seeking trouble with no man, least of all Cole Logan. But it strikes me there's times when

Cole does push a little too hard on his end of the rope. After all, he's just a two-legged man, same as you or me."

"You could be right," Imbaugh admitted. "Just the same, I can't see it as any part of your business or mine to try and argue the point with him. And when you think back, Cole ain't made too many mistakes."

The barge slithered on, slow but ponderously sure. The stage team tossed collective heads, stamped restlessly, anxious to be on solid earth again. When the ferry eased to its stop against the far bank and the apron thumped down, the animals hit their collars with a surge and snaked the stage clear. The driver braked to a new halt as one of the waiting riders threw up a challenging hand. The driver spat and nodded.

"Morning, Duff. Waco, how are you?"

Duff Twining was a leathery, tight-lipped rider. Waco Dart was stocky, with cheekbones so broad and high as to give his eyes a sort of upward, almost oriental slant. He was a burly brute. Duff Twining's voice held a harsh bite.

"Any passengers, Sage?"

"Some. He's one of them." Sage tipped his head toward Dan Scoville, who had moved up beside the stage, ready to board it again.

Twining gave Scoville a brief stare. "Where's the rest?"

The driver squirmed a trifle. "Inside."

"Would any of them be Bid Hazen?"

The driver squirmed again, then shrugged resignedly. "Yeah, Bid's in there—him and his missis." Then he added, with some show of truculence, "They got every right to ride my stage, same as anybody else who pays the fare."

Twining's bleak mouth pulled down. "Cole warned you against hauling those people back, Sage. He'll be speaking to you about that. But right now me and Waco will take care of Mister Hazen."

Twining gigged his horse, whirling it up beside the stage so abruptly that Dan Scoville had to side-step fast to keep from being trampled. He'd been listening and watching with increasing interest, and now, as he dodged Twining's fretting horse, the casual gleam in his eye turned frosty.

"Mister," he told Twining, "you're damned careless. Watch yourself!"

Duff Twining paid him no attention at all, but reached out and jerked open the door of the stage.

"All right, Hazen—come out of there!"

Waco Dart shifted his horse slightly, watching the door of the stage with slant-eyed intentness.

Sage, the driver, put up further argument. "This is a damned highhanded sort of business, Duff. Hope you're understanding that, even if Cole Logan did order it. Stopping my stage and pulling a legitimate passenger off it comes mighty close to being outright holdup. Better go slow!"

As he had with Dan Scoville's remark, Twining ignored Sage's warning. He lashed the stage's interior with a tone increasingly harsh.

"I'm not telling you again, Hazen. If I have to come in there after you, it'll be plenty tough and dirty. Show yourself!"

There was another moment of pause, broken by some low-toned protest on the part of Bid Hazen's wife. But right after that, Hazen showed in the door of the vehicle, thin face working. His glance flickered nervously about and, despite the morning's chill, a faint beading of sweat slimed his gaunt cheeks. His voice ran high and jerky.

"You can't make me get out, Twining. I got the right—"

Duff Twining leaned far out of his saddle, slashed a reaching arm, and locked clawing fingers in the front of Hazen's shirt.

"The hell I can't make you get out!"

Twining finished the words with a hauling yank, gigging his horse again at the same moment, spinning the animal away from the stage. Bid Hazen grabbed frantically at the stage door for support, missed it, and then came out headlong. And, as Twining let go his grip, the luckless Hazen slammed face down against the earth, where he lay in an ungainly sprawl, half stunned.

There was a thin cry of protest from within the stage, then Bid Hazen's wife showed at the door of the vehicle. "You leave him alone! You leave my man alone—!"

Twining never gave her a glance. He merely growled, "All right, Waco—work him over. He had one chance and he wouldn't listen. So he's asked for it. Make it good!"

Waco Dart stepped from his saddle, moved over to Bid Hazen with a rolling swagger, a small smile of anticipation on his lips, a cruel flicker in his eyes. He leaned down and hauled Hazen to his feet. His voice was a guttural purr.

"Now in a way you're lucky, Hazen. The orders could have been to hang you. As it is—"

Waco Dart hunched his right shoulder and drove a hammering fist into Bid Hazen's dazed and unprotected face. Hazen's knees buckled and he went down again. From the door of the stage came another protesting cry, part of it a dry sob.

"Leave my Bid alone—"

The gaunt, faded woman started to climb down from the stage. She stumbled, almost fell as she reached the ground.

Grizzled Joe Imbaugh looked at her, then turned with a growling, deep-throated protest, while Sage, the stage driver, cursed impotently from his perch up on the high box of the Concord. Dan Scoville swung his glance away from Waco Dart and the hapless Bid Hazen, laid it on Duff Twining.

"Enough of that sort of business," he rapped coldly. "Call your dog off!"

To all of this, Duff Twining showed complete indifference. He was leaning a little forward in his saddle, hands crossed on the horn, watching Waco Dart at his ruthless chore.

"Make it good, Waco," he droned. "Make it plenty good!"

Twining's right side was toward Dan Scoville, and he was but two short strides distant as he sat his saddle with such confident and callous unconcern. His gun sagged along his right thigh, butt flaring from the holster. That hint of pressure at Dan Scoville's lip corners grew suddenly more pronounced, and he was cat fast across the short interval of distance, grabbing at Twining's gun.

Startled, Twining blurted a curse and made a belated reach for the weapon, only to find Scoville's fist in the way. So then he caught at Scoville's wrist. There was a brief explosion of struggle, the advantage going to Scoville as he jerked his wrist free, Twining's gun solid in his hand.

Twining, cursing again, aimed a clubbing blow at Scoville's head, but Scoville slid inside the blow, locked his free hand in Twining's belt, and hauled him bodily from the saddle. Then, as Twining came spilling down, Scoville brought up a bunched and driving knee to meet him.

Twining's face and that hard knee met with a crunch, and then Twining was rolling on the ground, his senses knocked half out of him.

Waco Dart, intent on his manhandling of Bid Hazen, had bent over to haul Hazen back to his feet once more and set him up for further punishment. So, he was slow to react to the first flurry of struggle between Dan Scoville and Duff Twining. Now, as he jerked erect and swung around, half starting for his gun, he found Twining's horse between him and Scoville, which meant that, as a target, Scoville was virtually hidden, while he himself stood in the full open, with no protection at all. This realization slowed him in his reach for his gun. And then Scoville slid quickly into the clear and stared coldly at Waco along the barrel of Duff Twining's gun.

"I said enough of that business." The gun made a little stabbing move. "Back away and mind your manners! Forget any ideas about that gun of yours. You'd never get there!"

Scoville moved in on Waco. The gun made that stabbing flicker again. "Your hands," said Scoville. "I want to see them up even with your ears. Now!"

Waco blinked, a sluggish, malevolent anger blurring his pale, upslanted eyes. But his hands lifted.

"Better!" rapped Scoville. "Turn around!"

Waco turned, and Scoville stepped close behind

him and lifted away his gun, dropping the weapon into the side pocket of his coat. Then Scoville backed away a few strides. "Now," he said, "we'll have a little understanding, all around."

"Yeah," came Duff Twining's voice thickly, "we sure as hell will!"

Twining had got to his feet again, where he wavered a little unsteadily. He'd lost his hat, and a lock of lank hair fell forward across his forehead. His lips were mashed and cut, already swelling to a pout and seeping crimson. His eyes, seething, were riveted on Dan Scoville.

"Mister," he gritted, "you just made a bad mistake, a damn bad mistake. You butted into something that's none of your damn business. Now if you're aiming to ride this stage into Delta, that'll be another mistake. For, if you live, you'll crawl out of Delta on your hands and knees. If you live!"

The raw chill in Scoville's manner did not change. Holding Twining's glare, he shrugged. "So you say. I wouldn't count on it. Have a look at this."

He brushed back the flap of his coat. There, pinned to the breast of his flannel shirt, was a ball-pointed star.

"That's it. The name is Dan Scoville. I'm a deputy out of Sheriff Frank Ide's office in Riverton. I'm going to headquarter at this town of Delta. If you want to carry out that word on ahead, it's quite all right with me. Any more remarks?"

Duff Twining, steady on his feet again, eyed the disclosed badge of office for a long moment. "So that's it! I might have guessed." His glance lifted, to meet the boring chill of Scoville's eyes. "There'll be some to argue that angle with you, plenty!" He caught up his hat, moved over to his horse, mopping at his bloody mouth with his sleeve. "Come on, Waco. We're getting out of here."

Dan Scoville watched silently as they climbed into their saddles, set the spurs, and surged away, pounding up to the levee top and speeding out along it. When dust and distance hid them, he turned to Bid Hazen.

"Maybe you got an answer to what this is all about?"

Weak rage broke from Hazen. "Answer? Colc Logan, of course. Cole Logan, damn him! Setting himself up as the law of the land. Who does he think he is?"

Hazen scrubbed a hand across his beaten, bruised face, then resumed his nasal tirade.

"This is just another example of his way. You do as he says, you let him push you around, you bow your head when the great man rides by—or he kills you, or tries to run you out of the country. But he don't get away with that kind of business any more with me. I got my rights. I got just as many rights as him or any other man."

"That's right," admitted Scoville, "you have. And we'll see to it that those rights are respected." He looked up at Sage. "Ready to roll again?"

Sage nodded gravely. "We aim to get to Delta, we got to start some time." Sage swung his glance to Bid Hazen. "Sure you want to come along, Bid? Was I in your boots about now, I'd do a mite of serious thinking on the matter."

"I've done my thinking," blurted Hazen, shuffling unsteadily over to the stage door. "Me and the missis, we're going back to our shanty boat. It's our home. To hell with Cole Logan!"

Hazen climbed into the stage, brushing aside the protests of his wife, who climbed in behind him. "Marthy," Scoville heard him say, "it ain't no use to try and change my mind. I been telling you that, over and over. We're going back to what's ours and we're going to stay there. And if Cole Logan or anybody else of his outfit ever tries to come at me again, then I borrow a gun from Cat Jenson or one of the other folks—and I'll use it. That's final!"

The door slammed shut behind Hazen. Dan Scoville looked around at the others, at Joe Imbaugh and the half-breed. The latter had been staring at Scoville with no particular friendliness, and now his glance slid guardedly away. Joe Imbaugh cleared his throat.

"You handled things pretty neat just now,

mister—and I got to admit with pretty good cause. Yet I say this. I doubt you're going to like Delta or that Delta is going to like you. And I doubt that many folks are going to sit up and beg at sight of that star you're packing."

Scoville twitched a casual shoulder. "An opinion, friend," he conceded, "but only yours. We'll see."

The ferryman started to say something more, changed his mind, and headed for his shanty, the half-breed trailing at his heels. Scoville watched them for a moment, a musing light in his eyes. Then he put a foot on a wheel hub and drew himself up to the box of the Concord. "I'll ride the rest of the way with you, Sage."

Sage bobbed his head. "Suits you, suits me."

The stage racked past Imbaugh's shanty, climbed to the levee top, and rolled along into the eye of the rising sun. For some time there was silence, save for the dry squeak of the leather thoroughbraces as the body of the stage swung and rolled, and for the scrape and clack of the wheels and the muted mutter of hoofs in the dusty road. Dan Scoville's thoughts drifted back to his parting with Sheriff Frank Ide at Riverton.

"It could turn out to be a pretty tough assignment, Dan," Frank Ide had told him. "So I'm not going to tie your hands in any way with a lot of do's and don'ts. You've had enough experience at this game to know your way around, to know when to handle them easy and when to handle them rough. I'm not completely sold on the story that lawyer, George Delbert, had to tell, and nothing is truer than the old saying about there always being two sides to every story. But Delbert is a gabby one and he's been yapping to the county commissioners, and they're spurring me some about affairs on Middle Island. So I want you to go down to Delta, get the picture clear in your mind, and then, once and for all, put the animals in their proper stalls and make it stick! I'll back whatever moves you have to make, clear across the boards. Good luck!"

That, mused Dan Scoville, was the way Frank Ide had put it to him and that was the way he would play his cards. It was an uncertain game he faced and there was no telling what would turn up. But that was the spice in this kind of assignment, and there was a cool calm in him as he considered the future.

Beside him, swaying to the lift and jounce of the stage box, Sage ruminated over his cud of tobacco, holding to a studied silence. Scoville glanced at him, a faint gleam of sardonic amusement in his eyes.

"Don't tell me that sight of this star of mine has got you worried, too, friend? Back at the ferry, that half-breed in particular acted almost uneasy."

Sage grunted. "Mebbe with reason. I wouldn't

know and I care less. Me? No, I'm not worried. I'm just thinking."

"About what—if it's any of my business?"

Sage considered for another little time of silence, then shrugged and from behind a shielding hand spat a stream of amber juice into the roadside dust.

"I'll say this, and then keep my mouth shut. I'd remind you that appearances can be mighty deceiving. Now I don't take kindly to having my stage stood up by anybody, unless it's for strict, legitimate business reasons. I reckon you heard me tell Duff Twining that. No, sir—I don't take kindly to that sort of business, even when Cole Logan orders it. But past that point, well—" Sage let another shrug carry on the rest of his thought.

"I see," murmured Scoville. "Yes, I think I see. But everybody has certain rights. That applies to Bid Hazen, too."

"Maybe it does," admitted Sage. "We'll say that we agree on that. Still and all, it pays to have a look at all the angles. You look at just one part of a picture, and you get one idea. But then, when you see all the picture, like as not you'll get a complete different one. Now here's something you can bet on. When such as Bid Hazen gets in Cole Logan's shadow, then he measures up so damn small you can't hardly find him. Yes, sir—when you get all through adding up and subtracting from, that's the way it stands."

Dan Scoville reached for his pipe. "From what I heard back at the ferry, I gather you'll probably have a little argument with this Cole Logan hombre for hauling Hazen back to Delta."

"Shouldn't wonder," Sage nodded. "Which ain't worrying me none. Cole knows how far he can go with me. When it comes to who I do or don't haul on my stage, that's my business and I'll attend to it, and ask no permission or favors from anybody." Sage unloaded another mouthful of tobacco juice, then turned his head and fixed Scoville with a direct look.

"Friend, there's something about you that I like. So, while maybe you won't thank me for it, I'm going to give you a mite of real advice. Which is, don't make snap judgment on anybody in these parts. Because it's like this. For considerable time this stretch of country has been kind of like a little world all its own. Folks have handled things in their own way for so long they've got used to the habit. Now there'll be some who'll be glad to see that star of yours show up, and there'll be others who won't. But it'll pay you to remember that just because a man may not like the sight of your star too well, is no sign he ain't a pretty good man, all things considered."

Scoville's answer was dry. "Given a chance, I can generally get along with people. But I wouldn't be here if Sheriff Frank Ide didn't think it was necessary. And with good reason, from what I've seen so far."

"Oh, sure," conceded Sage. "That part's true enough. We got our bad ones as well as our good ones. What I'm driving at is that you'll show a lot of savvy if you take time to make damn sure just who is which."

Sage squared around again and flicked the off wheeler of his team with the whip.

"You, Barney! Put some weight into that collar. You ain't pulled more than half a lick all morning."

II—Delta

The town was just a huddle of low buildings, clinging to the south side of a curving levee. From the loft of this, plus that of the stage box, Dan Scoville could look down across the scatter of rooftops, and his thought was that here was as drab and uninviting a place as he had ever looked at.

On the north side of the levee lay the brown waters of Cross Over Slough, now giving off a brassy glitter under the sun. Jutting out a little way into the slough was a small wharf of sodden piling and worn, splintery planks, and on one corner of this a barefoot urchin squatted, patient over a dangling fishline. Scattered along this side of the levee also were several weathered shanties, and there were three or four ancient houseboats, moored to tree stumps by sagging, slime-coated ropes.

Ragged stands of tules fringed the slough waters, and above these the levee banks were clothed with willow and bay and sycamore trees, with an occasional swamp oak, and here and there the thicker foliage of a live oak lifted its solid bulk of cooling shadow. Over all hung a suggestion of isolation, of loneliness and lethargic existence.

Opposite the wharf the levee road dipped down to meet the town's single street, striking this about halfway along it. Sage made the abrupt turn into the street with easy, expert judgment, pulling up before the porch of a long, low building which housed a general store. As he set the brake and looped reins about it, Sage said gruffly:

"Well, here it is. Delta. I hope you'll like it and it'll like you, Deputy."

With that Sage leaned over, pulled a thin mail sack from under the seat, climbed down, and stamped across the porch into the store. Dan Scoville dropped down the other side of the Concord, went around to the rear of it, tossed back the leather cover of the luggage boot, and lifted out a sacked saddle and small canvas grip-sack, piling these items on the store porch.

The door of the stage opened and Bid Hazen peered out, his glance running nervously up and down the street before settling on Scoville. His words came hurried, a little feverish.

"You're a law man—you pack a star. I'm entitled to the protection of that star. You got to see that Cole Logan and his damn bully boys leave me alone. I got my rights, and—"

"Your rights will be looked after," cut in Scoville with some curtness. He'd started out feeling sorry for this man. Now he also knew a small edge of contempt, for there was very little about Bid Hazen to inspire respect. The man seemed a queer mixture of sulky stubbornness, of whining complaint, and now, jittery cowardice.

Hazen let himself down to the street, took another hurried look around, then scuttled into the store at a high-kneed shamble. Like nothing so much, thought Scoville, as a terrified rodent diving for the sanctuary of a burrow.

Hazen's gaunt, faded wife moved more slowly. Dan Scoville stepped up to give her a hand down from the stage, and a faint flush touched her worn face at this small gesture of gallantry.

"Thank you," she murmured. Then, looking Scoville steadily in the eye, she spoke her courageous lie. "Bid would have helped me, only he's so worried he was a mite forgetful."

Dan Scoville tipped his head slightly. "I'm sure of that, ma'am." He touched his hat and watched with grave respect as she followed her husband into the store.

Scoville himself seemed in no hurry for any particular destination. He had his own good look at the run of the street and what it held. Then his survey came back to the store and the building which held it. He walked along the porch, looking in at door and window. At one of these near the far end of the porch he paused for some time, cupping his hands about his eyes as he peered through the dusty, cobweb-festooned panes. Then he came back and worked at the tie of the sack which held his saddle. The sack held other things besides riding gear, among them being a cartridge belt and holstered gun.

A shade of deeper gravity touched his face as he strapped on the weapon, as though by this act he assumed a new personality and mantle of definite purpose. He had retied the sack and was just straightening up when hoofs beat at the eastern end of the street and four riders hove into view, coming at a fast lope.

Two of these Scoville recognized immediately. Duff Twining and Waco Dart. Of the other two riding out in front, one was a girl, slim and upright in divided skirt, blue blouse, and a flat-crowned Stetson. Dan Scoville's glance touched her briefly, instinctively approving her sure, straight-backed balance in the saddle. Then his survey moved over and fastened on the man riding beside her.

A man of about thirty, Scoville judged, and one who filled his saddle with a heavy-shouldered bigness. A slightly forward-leaning figure who seemed to throw a certain shadow of masterfulness ahead of him. There was a square and dominant jaw, a beaked and forceful nose, and coldly gray eyes burning out of a sun-blackened face.

Duff Twining, his glance raking the street, spurred up beside the big man, said something, then pointed at Dan Scoville. The big man angled his horse slightly and came straight in at the store, cutting past the stage and setting his mount up in a scattering of dust which splashed against the low porch edge, with some of it reaching far enough to add another coating to Scoville's already dusty boots. The move might not have been calculated, but the effect was the same, and a faint burn of color seeped across Scoville's face.

"Mister," he said, "you almost make the earth shake. Remember, I said—almost."

The big man stared, unwinking and arrogant. His voice was a growl. "Sure this is him, Duff?"

"That's him, Cole."

Dan Scoville noted that both Duff Twining and Waco Dart were armed again, so he gave them just enough of his attention to keep them placed. The big man shot his next question directly at Scoville.

"What have you done with Bid Hazen? I want to know, and I'm Cole Logan."

Dan Scoville would have been less than human if the weight of this man's tone and manner hadn't got under his skin somewhat. So now there was a barb of crisp sarcasm in his answer.

"Cole Logan, eh? What am I supposed to do, fall flat on my face?"

This curt jibe hit home. Cole Logan leaned a little forward in his saddle. "You can save the smart talk. What have you done with Bid Hazen?"

Scoville shrugged. "What gives you the idea that I'd do anything with him?"

Logan was heavily insistent. "Where is he?"

Scoville shrugged again, letting it go at that, fighting back the slow burn of anger kept smoldering by this fellow's rough arrogance. Cole Logan pulled around in his saddle, jerked his head in a commanding nod.

"Take a look in the store, Duff. Hazen's probably in there, aiming to hide behind Bill Profitt. If he's there, drag him out here!"

Twining obediently stepped from his saddle and moved up on the porch, where he found Dan Scoville between him and the door. Scoville's voice took on a deceptive softness.

"Now let's not get violent about anything. Maybe Hazen is in the store. But I don't like this talk of dragging people around, and until I've been shown a lot better cause to the contrary than any I've seen so far, Hazen can stay in the store or leave it, as he pleases. And he's not going to be dragged or kicked around by you or anybody else. Is that clear?"

Cole Logan's voice rang harshly. "Waco, get down there with Duff. Push this fool aside and go get Hazen."

Dan Scoville rolled up slightly on his toes, and now, abruptly, there was no softness in his tone at all.

"Everybody stay put!" Scoville's glance bored

at Cole Logan. "What are you so damned proud about? How tall do you think you stand? You want some dead men in this street? Well, you'll see some there if you don't back up and walk a little softer! I suggest that the lady move away. This is no place for her if you're bound to have this thing come up rough."

The girl answered in her own way. She was lithely quick out of the saddle and up on the porch, her back to Scoville, her face to Cole Logan. Her words ran crisp.

"Cole, come to your senses! Can't you see that this man isn't to be bluffed or bullied? Duff told you he carried a star, so he's entitled to know what this is all about. Why don't you tell him?"

"Now," put in Scoville, his tone smoothing out again, "that makes reason. If you got a legitimate charge against this Bid Hazen for some kind of criminal action, and you want to make a regular complaint through the proper channels, then I'll slap an arrest on him and see that he stands trial at Riverton. Well?"

Increasing anger built up darkly in Cole Logan's face. Also, it seemed to Scoville, there was a shade of uncertainty momentarily reflected. But a black and stubborn pride was dominant over everything. Logan shot a curt order at the girl.

"Nora, you keep out of this! I can handle—"

"No!" cut in the girl spiritedly, "no, you can't

handle this affair the way you usually do. And no miserable shanty-boat meat thief is worth starting violence over. I won't move a step from here until you promise to talk sense."

Cole Logan glared angrily at her for a moment, then his fuming glance shifted again to Scoville.

"All right. You heard what Nora Baine just called Hazen. A meat thief. That's what he is, a damned slow-elker. I ran him off this island once. I had plenty of good cause to hang him, but for the sake of his wife I gave him another chance. I told him to get out and not come back, and that if he tried to return, then he'd get the rope treatment, for sure. So—now—!"

Dan Scoville shook his head. "No—not so now. It will be like I said. If you figure you got a legitimate criminal charge against Hazen, and will swear to it, then I'll see that the law decides matters. Otherwise, Hazen isn't going to be bothered."

Cole Logan slammed a clenched fist on his saddle horn. "Hell with your puling law! I don't go for that at all. While he lived, my father was the law on Middle Island. Before him, my grandfather was the same. Now, I'm the law! You go on back to Riverton, mister, and let us handle our own affairs in our own way."

Through slightly pinched eyes, Dan Scoville studied this man, this Cole Logan. For, though Logan's words suggested an almost fantastic conceit and arrogance, it was Scoville's feeling that these were not all the answers. This man spoke as though swayed by a deep and utterly sincere conviction. Like a man might speak who felt that a certain destiny, or duty, had been handed down to him, and who believed utterly in that obligation. It was a strange and disquieting thing, and disturbing in its implications. Scoville made another attempt at reason.

"Man, you can't mean that. Open your mind to common sense. Middle Island is a part of a county that is subject to the authority of Sheriff Frank Ide's office, not to any imagined authority of yours. For a third time I say that if you've anything real to accuse Hazen of, then Frank Ide's office will take care of him. But if you haven't, then he's free to come and go as he pleases, without fear of you or any other man. And I'm here to see that just that basic right is maintained."

Blue eyes and gray ones, both bleak, both chill, locked and held. It was finally Cole Logan's glance which flickered and slid away. The big man seemed struck with uncertainty and confusion of a sort. As though, for the first time, an accepted tenet of his entire existence had been challenged by the unswerving authority of constituted law. It was a situation which demanded a whole new set of answers, and just now Cole Logan did not have those answers. It was something he had to do some thinking on. Bewilderment was in the swing of his head, baffled anger in his voice as he made concession, while also maintaining a wall of defiance.

"I can wait. Bid Hazen can't stay in that store or in this town forever. I'll get my chance to pick him up, and when I do, then he hangs! You got my word on that, law man."

"In that case," answered Dan Scoville, equally adamant, "I'll be coming for you, Logan. I'll put an arrest on you and take you to Riverton to answer to the court. And I'll take you, dead or alive! Does that answer you?"

For the first time the domineering harshness of Cole Logan's face showed a slight break. The shadow of a mirthless smile quirked his lips.

"So you'd come after me, would you? There's the elements of a good belly laugh in that prospect. Yeah, a good one. Only—the laugh wouldn't be yours." He twisted in the saddle, jerked his head. "All right, Duff—hit leather. We're getting out of here. Come along, Nora. This time you win."

The girl shook her head. "No, Cole. Your tone is wrong and so is your manner. I'm staying in town until I'm ready to leave of my own accord."

Logan stared at her, made as if to speak, shrugged instead. He spun his horse abruptly, headed out, Waco Dart falling in beside him. Duff Twining, moving reluctantly, swung into his saddle, then looked cold-eyed at Dan Scoville.

"Mister, you got no idea how unpopular you're due to be around here. You just got no idea at all!"

Scoville's smile was faint, sardonic. "Yours, I believe," he said. "And this one is Mister Dart's. Take them with my compliments. Catch!"

One after the other he pulled from his coat pockets the guns he'd taken off Twining and Waco Dart back at the Spanish Slough ferry. He tossed them to Twining, who, in his surprise, barely managed to catch them. Now, with a gun in each hand, Twining stared at Scoville, plainly puzzled, unable to figure the real worth of this man of the law.

"I'm wondering," said Twining flatly, "how much is bluff and how much is salt? I reckon time will answer that."

He rode away, after Cole Logan and Waco Dart.

Now it was Dan Scoville's turn to be startled, for the girl turned and faced him and spoke crisply. "Cole Logan wasn't the least bit afraid of you. I hope you realize that."

It was Scoville's thought that she was nice to look at. She had brown hair and eyes and her cheeks were smooth and sun-tanned. She reflected a direct and wholesome vigor, and there was an antagonistic challenge in every graceful line of her. Before Scoville could figure out an answer to her blunt statement, she spoke again.

"Cole Logan is also an honest man, while Bid Hazen is just another cheap thief."

Dan Scoville tipped his head, slight irony in his words. "All that may be so. Thanks for telling me."

She either missed the irony, or chose to pay it no attention. "I just wanted to put you right on those things, for it will pay you to remember them in the future."

"Now," murmured Scoville, "that sounds almost like a threat. Or is it advice? Everybody seems to want to give me advice."

"Perhaps," she retorted curtly, "you'll find that you need it."

She turned then, and went into the store, and Dan Scoville, after a short moment, followed her.

It was a cluttered yet orderly place, this store. With shadowed corners and with its walls and beams soaked with an odor which combined the pleasant pungencies of smoked bacon and of coffee and the spice of pepper. There was the savor of dried onions, the smell of cloth and drygoods, of boot and saddle and harness leather, and of beeswax and tobacco.

In a far corner Bid Hazen lurked, uneasy and watchful, his gaunt wife patient beside him. At the counter the stage driver and another man stood talking to Bill Profitt, the storekeeper. It was a low-toned group which broke up as the girl, then Dan Scoville, entered. Sage, the stage driver, turned and headed out, boot heels clumping. As he passed Dan Scoville, he dropped a small murmur.

"That was pretty fair for a start out there, friend. But don't let it make you too proud."

The storekeeper spoke with a slightly nasal twang. "Morning, Nora. If you're looking for Molly, she's out back."

The girl nodded. "Thanks, Bill."

As she headed for the shadowy rear of the place, the man across the counter from Bill Profitt spoke, touching his hat.

"Nora, how are you?"

Standing quietly, watching and listening, it seemed to Dan Scoville that the girl's head lifted a trifle higher, that her slim shoulders went a little straighter, while her voice ran cool and brittle.

"How do you do, Mister Requa."

Then she was past, the sound of her quick steps dwindling. A door opened and closed, and a small moment of complete silence lay across the store. Dan Scoville broke this by moving up to the counter, his glance centering on Bill Profitt.

"You own this building, maybe?"

Bill Profitt nodded slowly. He was a thin, angular man, with a long, bony face and shrewd, slightly squinted eyes. He studied Dan Scoville gravely. "That's right, I do. What about it?"

"Why," said Scoville, "I noticed that there's a corner room to the place that might have been an office of some kind at one time. Right now it seems to be vacant. If that's so, then maybe you and me might get together and make a deal on it."

"What kind of a deal?"

"You might rent it to me. I'm Dan Scoville, a deputy from Sheriff Frank Ide's office in Riverton. Ide sent me down here to set up an office."

The storekeeper was silent for a moment, considering. "It used to be an office, all right," he conceded finally. "It was George Delbert's law office until he pulled stakes. There's two rooms, front and back. But I don't know about renting them to you."

"Why don't you know?" countered Scoville levelly.

Profitt rubbed a forefinger up and down beside his nose, while giving Scoville another moment of careful scrutiny. "It wouldn't be worth the time and trouble if you're only going to stay a few days."

The implication was plain, and a glint of frost built up in Scoville's eyes. "You needn't worry. I don't scare that easy."

"Cole Logan ain't done with you."

"And I'm not done with him," shot back Scoville. "Well, how about it? Do I get those rooms or do I locate somewhere else in town?"

Bill Profitt considered a moment longer, then shrugged. "Your funeral. If you can stand it, I reckon I can. We'll take a look at the rooms, and if they suit you, why then I guess we can hit it off. The name is Scoville, you say? Well, I'm Bill Profitt and this is Ward Requa." He followed his words with a nod toward his companion.

Dan Scoville shook hands with both of them. Ward Requa was a solidly built man, swarthy of skin, with quick, dark eyes and a slightly twisted mouth, which gave the impression that here was one who was constantly and somewhat cynically amused at the world and all that it held. His handshake was firm and brisk.

"To say I'm happy to know you, Scoville, is putting it mildly."

"Yes? How's that?"

Requa shrugged, his small, cynical smile widening a trifle. "Wait a few weeks and then ask that question. By that time you'll be able to answer it yourself, I suspect."

The door to the empty law office was unlocked and Bill Profitt opened it wide. In the front room there was a somewhat battered, but still sound table, with several round-backed chairs. The rear room held an iron bunk with bare springs, an old bureau, and another chair. There was plenty of dust and cobwebs in the corners and on the windows, and the paint on the walls and ceiling, thinly spread in the first place, had faded to a neutral drabness.

"Could stand a good mucking out," said Bill Profitt, somewhat apologetically. "But after George Delbert left I just sorta let things slide in here. I'll throw in some gear for that bunk, a washbowl and pitcher, and Molly's got an extra looking glass to go on top of that bureau yonder. Whole layout is yours for fifteen dollars a month."

Dan Scoville nodded quickly. "I'll pay you a couple of months in advance."

Bill Profitt gave him a short, quick stare. "You sure do aim to stick, don't you? Well, there's no rush about paying, but if you want it that way, it's all right with me. Now I'll go rustle that bed gear for you and send somebody to do the sweeping out and brushing down."

The storekeeper went out, but Ward Requa lingered, twisting up a brown paper cigarette. He proffered the makings to Scoville, who accepted with a nod. Requa touched a match to his cigarette, inhaled deeply, and said, "I want to show you something, friend."

He led the way to the front room, stepped over to the inner wall, and touched a spot there. The spot was a bullet hole.

"A forty-five," drawled Requa. "Went plumb through this wall and ended up puncturing a can of 'air-tights' on one of Bill Profitt's shelves.

Also, the main reason for George Delbert pulling out."

Dan Scoville studied the bullet hole for a moment, then swung his glance to meet Ward Requa's sardonic eyes. "Should I be interested? Or is this maybe meant for a threat?"

Requa's shoulders shook silently with inner laughter. "Lord love you, man—of course not! But this is a strange country, Scoville—with strange people in it. I pointed out that bullet hole just as a friendly hint. So you won't sit under a light on a dark night in line with a window or with your door open, now that you've had your little run-in with Cole Logan. That's what George Delbert did after he'd rowed with Logan a couple of times. And that slug came close to parting George's hair."

"What did they row about?" asked Scoville.

Requa pursed his lips, blew the ash off his cigarette. "George took the written law pretty seriously. Certain people brought their troubles to George, figuring that through him the law would take care of their rights. George felt that way about it, too. Cole Logan didn't, so he and George argued the point a few times."

"Does that suggest that Logan had anything to do with the shot that put this bullet hole here?"

Again Ward Requa's shoulders shook with that silent inner laughter. "Another question I'll let time answer for you. You've already met up with Cole Logan and a couple of his men. Wait until you've had a look at the whole Logan tribe. Uncle Tobe, for instance. And cousin Rack. By all means you got to meet cousin Rack. And then there's the beautiful and haughty Loren, Cole's sister. I tell you, Scoville, you got to really know the Logans to understand a lot of things. Well, I'll be seeing you around."

Ward Requa went out, and the sound of his boot heels dwindled down the store porch. Dan Scoville got out his pipe and puffed soberly, his glance again touching that bullet hole in the wall.

III—Digging In

It was the same youngster Dan Scoville had seen fishing off the wharf, just before the stage had turned down from the levee road into town. He carried a broom in one hand and a bucket of water and several rags in the other.

"I'm Tod Neely," he said. "Bill Profitt sent me to sort of clean things up in here, Mister Scoville."

He had boyhood's hipless lankiness and boyhood's love of the sun burned into him with a deep brownness. His face was thin, his eyes very clear and blue and a little shy. It was plain that he wore his flimsy cotton shirt and faded bib overalls only because convention demanded that he be clothed, not because he felt that anything more than warm sunshine was really necessary. His bare, brown feet padded softly on the floor. He was twelve years old, and there was a considerable amount of awe in the glance he put on Dan Scoville's star.

"You're a law man, ain't you, Mister Scoville?"

Scoville grinned at him. "That's right, Tod. You approve?"

The boy seemed to consider this soberly before nodding. "This country needs a law man, I guess. If you'd been here a couple of years ago, then I reckon my pap would still be alive."

Scoville's grin faded. "How do you figure that, Tod?"

Setting down the bucket of water and the rags, the youngster went after the dust and cobwebs, wielding the broom a trifle fiercely. "Because then you'd have showed Cole Logan that he ain't God Almighty!"

Scoville studied the lad for a quiet moment. "You mean that Cole Logan had something to do with the death of your father, Tod?"

The boy ceased swinging the broom, stood quiet, staring out the open door. "Mebbe not exactly Cole Logan. But some of his crowd, I reckon. More'n likely it could have been Rack Logan. Leastways, that's what everybody figures."

"Who is everybody, Tod?"

The boy scuffed a bare foot against the floor. "Well, Maze Dickson for one and Ward Requa for another. And me, I figure that way, too."

"Anybody else, Tod?"

"I dunno for sure. But I reckon so. Folks generally figure that when some kind of rough business has took place, then it's Cole Logan or some of his outfit who done it."

"How did your father die, Tod?"

The boy's stare dropped to the floor and his voice ran low. "He was found floatin' in Cross Over Slough. There was a bullet hole in him and a rope around his neck."

Dan Scoville dropped a hand on the boy's thin shoulder. "That was pretty rough all right, Tod. But why should Cole Logan, or anybody else have treated your father that way?"

The boy's head came up and his blue eyes blazed. "Cole Logan accused my pap of stealin' Block L beef. With my own ears I heard him accuse Pap of that. But Cole Logan lied! My pap never stole nothin' from nobody—not ever!"

Steps sounded on the porch outside, and Tod Neely got busy with his broom again. Bill Profitt came in, carrying an armful of blankets and an empty canvas bedtick. He dropped these on the bunk.

"When you get through swamping out, Tod, then you take this bedtick down to Ed Jethro's livery barn and fill it with fresh, clean straw." Profitt turned to Scoville. "Things ought to shake down pretty comfortable for you here."

Scoville nodded. "Perfect for my needs."

Bill Profitt grinned faintly. "Told Molly about it and she likes the idea fine. She'll probably be showing up after a while to see that you're comfortable and that everything is clean. Molly's mighty strict about things being clean. You hear that, Tod? If you don't want Missis Profitt snatching you bald-headed, you do a first-class job of tidying up."

Bill Profitt went out again, and while Tod Neely worked with the broom, Dan Scoville took the bucket of water and the rags and got busy on the windows. From time to time he stole a glance at the boy.

A likable, appealing sort of a kid, he decided. But one who had already known a pretty savage mauling by life. Scoville wondered how long a thing like that might stay with a boy. . . .

It took them a good hour to clean up. Then Tod Neely took the bedtick and trotted off downstreet with it, coming back a little later with the straw-filled tick bulky and bulging across his shoulder. He helped Scoville spread and punch the tick into shape on the bunk, and then Scoville spread the blankets.

"Guess that does it, Tod," he said cheerfully. "And you've sure earned the right to come in here and make yourself at home any time you're a mind to."

The boy's eyes shone. "Thanks a heap, Mr. Scoville. I do my sleepin' in Maze Dickson's houseboat. I'll be seeing you around, though."

"Fine! And, Tod—forget the 'Mister.' Make it plain Dan."

For the first time a hint of a boyish smile showed through the settled gravity of the lad's thin face. He paused for a moment in the door. "All right, Dan." Then he pattered away.

Scoville brought in his sacked saddle and gripsack. From the latter he was taking a meager outlay of extra clothes and storing these in the bureau drawer when a woman's round and cheerful voice sounded.

"May I come in?"

She was a matronly soul, with quick, merry eyes and a kindly face under a crown of snowy hair.

"I'm Molly Profitt," she said. "And you're Dan Scoville, of course. Did that scamp of a Tod Neely do a good job of cleaning up? George Delbert, who had these rooms before, well, he might have been a good lawyer, but I swear he was the most untidy man I ever saw."

She was moving around as she spoke, her quick eyes missing nothing. She finally nodded her approval. "It will do, all except this bare floor. I just can't abide a bare floor, so I'll be bringing in a couple of extra rag rugs that I have. When a man gets up in the morning, he shouldn't be asked to put his feet on a bare floor."

Scoville grinned. "No need of that, Mrs. Profitt. I'm not used to luxury."

Molly Profitt squared around to face him, hands on her ample hips. "Young man, you and that star of yours represent something this stretch of country has been in need of for a long time. Now that you're finally here, we want to make sure that you'll like us, so you'll stay."

"Seems to be a little mixed opinion on that," drawled Scoville. "About folks wanting me to stay, I mean."

"I know," nodded Molly Profitt. "Had some words with Cole Logan, didn't you?"

"Some."

"You'll have more, no doubt. A very stubborn man, Cole is, and so sure he's always right. The day he's finally made to understand that the law is the will of all the people, not just that of Cole Logan, well—that will be a great day all around. Be good for Cole, too."

"You think that can be done—convincing Logan, I mean?"

Her glance turned slightly grave. "I'm hoping so, Dan Scoville. And that it can be done without violence."

"That," said Scoville, equally grave, "I subscribe to, myself." He was thoughtful for a moment. "I never met up with anything like this before. In a way, the man is almost preposterous, yet when I was having it out with him I had the feeling that he was quite sincere in what he said and in his belief in himself."

"He is," nodded Molly Profitt. "And that is the frightening part of it. If it were all just a pose, to serve his own ends, then the stern hand of real authority might whip him into line without too much trouble. But as it is—" She sighed deeply. "Well, I'll go locate those rugs for you. And a lamp, too—you'll need a lamp."

She hurried off, and Dan Scoville went out on the porch in front of his new office. He got out his pipe and puffed soberly as he let his glance sift over what he could see of this town of Delta and of the long run of country out beyond it. And he thought of how deceptive appearances could be.

He'd never seen a more sleepy, indolent, apparently peaceful town. Yet, in the few short hours he'd been here he'd already run into a tangle of crosscurrents of opinion, along with items of information which carried a somber shadow of violence already done and the hint of more of the same in the offing.

A step sounded at the door of the store. It was Bid Hazen, his gaunt wife at his shoulder. Hazen looked at Scoville, but said nothing. Then his glance ran up and down the street with a long cautiousness before he finally came fully from the store and went along the porch to the far end. Here he paused for another survey all around, then slipped past the corner of the building and was gone, his wife a faithful shadow.

There was a high degree of furtiveness in Bid Hazen's every move. Either, mused Scoville, this Hazen was just a poor devil, hagridden with fear, or he was a pretty shifty customer. But who was to be the judge of that, either way? Local opinions couldn't be relied upon too much, for they differed radically on many things, it seemed.

He would, decided Scoville, have to wait and move slowly and form his own sure judgment and opinion on all men and their motives and actions. He'd be a fool to jump at any one man's notion. And there could be no taking of sides. He had to play this deal straight up and down the middle, favoring no man above another, while making the authority of his office stand up to all it represented. Which would be the law, fair and unbiased, with no preconceived judgment for or against anyone.

He knocked the dottle from his pipe and turned back into the office. His glance ran around the room and came to rest on a spot on the inner wall, a spot where a bullet had struck and gone through, a bullet hole which Ward Requa had pointed out to him. He moved over and was touching the spot with a probing forefinger when Nora Baine's voice sounded at the door behind him.

"That's the shot which hastened George Delbert's departure, so they say. What else did they tell you about it?"

Scoville turned slowly. She had a trim shoulder point against the doorpost and she leaned there, studying him with speculative intentness.

"What," asked Scoville, "makes you think anybody told me anything about it?"

"I know people and I know how the talk runs," she answered crisply. "Mind if I come in?"

Scoville tipped a lean head. "A pleasure. A chair?"

She moved into the room and sat down. Scoville took a chair across the table from her, wondering guardedly about this. He stoked his pipe anew, then waited.

Her glance was very direct and she was silent for some little time. Holding her glance, Scoville thought again that she was nice to look at, and she seemed to read his thought, for the tint of deepening color stole through her cheeks. Then she spoke abruptly.

"I'm afraid that in your way you're going to be just as stubborn as he is."

"He?"

"You know very well who I mean. Cole Logan, of course. And I just don't know what I'm going to do with the pair of you."

A thread of amusement flickered in Scoville's eyes. "And you feel that you have to try and do something?"

"Very definitely," she declared. "Somebody must." Abruptly much of the brisk self-assurance fell away from her and there was sober appeal in her manner. "You're going to have to help me in this, Dan Scoville."

He stirred in his chair. "In what way?"

"By making allowances and trying to understand why Cole is like he is."

"That's not easy," countered Scoville quietly. "A thing makes sense, or it doesn't. And Logan's pose of power doesn't make sense. We're not talking about a kid, playing at make-believe. We're speaking of a man grown, old enough to know better. And when a man like that comes roaring and ranting and making a lot of pretty serious threats, you hardly feel like handling him with kid gloves."

Nora Baine nodded. "I know. Yet—there are circumstances that should be considered."

"What kind of circumstances? Suppose you tell me all about it?"

For a little while she was silent, looking both at Scoville and past him.

"It starts a long way back," she said presently. "It began when the first of the Logans settled on Middle Island, which was before the island even had a name. The first Logans were among the earliest to come across the plains to California. The gold madness did not touch them particularly, but wide, free land to be had virtually for the asking did. They settled here on this island. They worked hard, did really tremendous things. They built levees against the threat of flood waters. They accumulated cattle and horse herds, set up the big Block L ranch, earned by the right of possession."

She paused, frowning a little, getting her thoughts and the picture straight, as she understood these things. Scoville ran a freshening match across the bowl of his pipe, waiting for her to go on. She cleared her throat.

"The Logans knew they could not keep the entire island to themselves forever. They knew that other people were bound to move in on it, and they had no objections to that, so long as the new arrivals were good, sound people. But another kind moved in, also. Undesirables, riff-raff of a frontier, ruffians fleeing the wrath of miners' courts and vigilante committees. A lot of these headed into this delta region to hide out. It wasn't long before, in one way or another, this element began to prey on the Logans, killing Logan cattle for food, stealing Logan horses and swimming these across the sloughs and selling them on the outside. In sheer self-defense the Logans had to fight back, smash this outlaw element and keep it smashed."

She darted a quick glance at Dan Scoville's grave, noncommittal face. "Is all this boring you?"

Scoville shook his head. "To the contrary. I'm very interested. Go on."

"Very well. Out of these early clashes with an outlaw element came the Logan tradition of enforcing certain fundamental laws on Middle Island, a responsibility which lesser men were quite content to leave in Logan hands. For the most part, it hasn't been too bad an idea—it has worked out satisfactorily in the eyes of most people. So—that is the way it has gone, a tradition of responsibility handed down across the years to the present time. Cole's grandfather and his father both assumed that responsibility, and in turn he's accepted it. I've told you all this so you might understand why Cole feels as he does."

Dan Scoville spoke slowly. "I can see why things should have been that way in the early days—why it was necessary and a good thing. But this is a different age, Miss Baine. Now we have regularly constituted law. So, what was necessary and probably admissible then is not so now."

"That is quite true," she admitted. "I'm not arguing the rightness of your position or stand. What I'm trying to do is give you a clear understanding of why Cole is like he is, so you'll show all the patience possible in trying to bring him to—to his senses."

There was, thought Scoville, the light of pleading in her eyes now. For she was seeing the inevitable clash between two sources of authority, one self-assumed, the other formulated and written by the will and needs of all men. And she was afraid of the outcome of that clash. Again Scoville stirred in his chair. He didn't want to hurt this girl, but facts were facts.

"Authority can be great, Nora Baine. But it can also turn dangerous, because authority means power and power can become a disease. Offhand, I say the disease had already touched Cole Logan."

She nodded, and her voice ran very low. "Yes, it has. And that is what makes me afraid. I am not so very old, but I understand the make-up of men pretty well, I think. And out there in the street a little while ago when you and Cole first faced each other, I could see that an issue between the two of you was definitely set. You had a gun and he had a gun and, while it did not come to that—" She faltered, biting her lip. "Dan Scoville, it must never come to that between you and Cole."

Scoville got to his feet, took a turn up and down the room, a lean and competent man, spokesman for the law of all men. Past the words of this girl—and there was a fine candor and honesty in her—he could see one plain fact. This girl was arguing with her heart as well as her mind. He came around and faced her gravely, touching the star on his shirt.

"What this represents has got to be the final authority on this island, Miss Baine. Cole Logan, as well as everyone else, is going to have to understand that. Just as you are, I'm hoping that bringing him to that understanding won't prove too difficult. But in the long picture, he's going to have to!" His tone softened. "This I'll promise you. I'll meet Cole Logan more than halfway and fairly in all things, and perhaps between the two of us we can cure him of this power disease." He smiled as he finished.

She stood up and moved to the door. There

she came around, searching Dan Scoville's face carefully again. She nodded, as though finally convinced of something.

"You're fair—and kind. Thank you, Dan Scoville. And I know you'll hold this talk in confidence."

"Of course." He moved over, smiling down at her. "I hope you don't mind my saying that Cole Logan has a very appealing and convincing champion."

Color welled up the smooth brown column of her throat, and she smiled in return. "I came in here convinced that I was probably going to end up disliking you completely, Dan Scoville. I was wrong. Thank you again for listening and understanding."

He watched her cross the porch to her horse, watched her ride out of town. Then he turned back and was considering what the rest of the day might hold for him when he heard again Molly Profitt's step. She came in, a small kerosene lamp in one hand, a couple of rag rugs over her other arm. She threw Scoville a shrewd glance.

"I hope you were nice to Nora Baine—for she's a fine girl. I hope she convinced you."

"Convinced me of—what?" drawled Scoville. "That she was a nice girl? She didn't have to try. I knew that the moment I saw her."

Molly Profitt set the lamp on the table, dropped the rugs to the floor. "Young man, don't look so innocent. Neither you nor Nora are fooling me one bit. I know why she came in to see you. The child was nervous as a kitten. She foresees plenty of clash between you and Cole Logan and she doesn't want it ever to come to a dangerous stage. I hope you gave her some comfort. She's arguing for the man of her heart, you know."

"I guessed that she was," admitted Scoville. "Lucky man—Cole Logan."

"Very," agreed Molly Profitt, "if he'll only get over his fool obsession in time to realize it." Then, in her cheerful, practical way she added, "Like any other mortal, you're going to have to eat. You may have noticed there's a little eating house across the street. I recommend it to you. Nell Tyce runs it and she serves very good food at fair prices. Later on, when I'm convinced you're the kind of man I think you are, I'll probably have you in every now and then to eat with Bill and me."

"That," smiled Scoville, "is a reward I'll work hard to deserve. When I first saw it I had no idea this town would hold so many nice womenfolk."

Molly Profitt laughed. "Away with your blarney! Now I'd better get out of here before folks start thinking that you hold some sort of fatal attraction for we womenfolk, Dan Scoville."

Mrs. Nell Tyce was a gaunt and tired-looking woman with sad eyes. She was both cook and waitress in her little eating house. But the place was clean and the food all that Molly Profitt said it would be, and Dan Scoville enjoyed his noon meal to the full. Several other men came in to eat and, while their main concern was food, Scoville felt the measuring glances of all of them, though they stayed strictly apart from him.

A couple of these were cowhands, lean, taciturn fellows. The others were of another type, men with the smell of slough waters on them, with a certain soft-fleshed slothfulness about them, which suggested a great deal of lazy, indolent living about them. Men of the slough-side shanties and moss-fouled shanty boats. These in particular eyed Scoville furtively. One of them, with a veined face and unshaven jowls, coming in late, took the second stool away from Scoville along the little counter. A sweat-stained undershirt covered his round and sloping shoulders and bulging belly, and his ragged and equally dirty jeans were held up by a belt of rope. He gave off the reek of cheap whiskey.

The two cowhands, finishing their meal, paid their score and moved to leave. One of them paused behind the man in the dirty undershirt and spoke with curt sarcasm.

"Eating honest beef for a change, eh, Dickson? I'd think you'd choke on it."

The fellow turned on his stool, scowling. "You mind your business, Potter—and I'll mind mine," he retorted thickly. "You got no cause to rawhide me. Maybe you don't know it, but the day is past when you saddle-pounders can act so damn high and mighty on this island. Something rode into Delta this morning on the stage. It's sittin' right next to me. The law."

The cowboy laughed with deepening sarcasm. "Heard about that. Well, that's fine. Suits me, all right. For I just can't imagine your breed snugglin' up to the law and getting anywhere. In your boots, I'd begin to scare."

The cowboy and his partner went on out, boot heels clicking, spurs chuffing musically.

Dan Scoville acted as though he hadn't heard a thing. But his thought was that here it was again. That crosscurrent of antagonisms and opinions. If he cared to look for them, he could pick up any amount of charges and countercharges; and some of them would be true and some of them otherwise. It would pay him to listen, of course, but he had to be very sure of one thing. And that was to form his final opinions and conclusions on what he saw, not on what he might hear.

From the eating house, Scoville went down along the street to where a corral ran a ragged rectangle and a livery barn with a paint-scabbed false front seemed to spraddle its ancient walls as though weary of holding up the roof. The old Concord stage, its bare tongue propped up on an empty nail keg, stood beside the stable. In the shade of the overhang, Sage the stage driver, and Ed Jethro the stable owner, squatted on their heels and traded meager talk. They quieted as Scoville came up to them.

“I’m going to need a horse,” said Scoville casually. “What’s the chances of getting one?”

Ed Jethro was a spry little cricket of a man, with an earthy, neutral look about him. He spoke in a reedy voice. “Rent or buy?”

“Depends on the horse—and the price,” answered Scoville with a faint smile.

“Out back,” said Jethro, leading the way.

They went around there, Sage falling into step with Scoville. “Looks like you’re diggin’ in for quite a stay,” observed Sage.

Scoville threw him a quick glance. “Did you think it would be otherwise?”

Sage hunched a shoulder. “Wasn’t sure at first. But,” he added, with a small grin, “you’re gettin’ a more solid look to you all the time.”

There was a scatter of horses in the corral, and Ed Jethro waved an encompassing hand. “Any of them,” he twanged thinly. “Take your choice. But the best of the lot is that claybank gelding. Honest bronc, fast, and with plenty of bottom.”

“Catch it up and we’ll have a close look,” said Scoville.

Jethro lifted a halter off a corral post, climbed in.

From here, at an angle past the shoulder of

another building, there was a clear view of the front of Bill Profitt's store. On the porch there, Bill Profitt stood talking to the two cowhands Scoville had seen in the eating house. Scoville jerked an indicating head.

"Those two yonder, Sage—talking to Profitt. Who are they?"

"Dick Potter and Curt Strang," informed Sage. "Circle Cross boys. That's Mal Baine's outfit. Salty scoundrels, but sound. You know 'em, you'll like 'em."

Ed Jethro brought the claybank gelding up to the corral fence, and Scoville climbed over and checked the animal, a move that made the little stable owner bristle slightly.

"I ain't no damn skinflint bronc trader. I say a horse is a good one, then it is."

"Sure," soothed Scoville. "I know that. But I just wanted a close-up look at the horse I'm going to buy. How much?"

Jethro named the price and it was a fair one, for Scoville could see that the animal was all Jethro claimed for it.

"You've sold a horse," said Scoville. "Make me out a bill of sale. I'll be leaving the animal here when not in use and I'll pay you whatever the stable and corral fee is."

They moved around in front of the stable again, and while Ed Jethro went inside to write out the bill of sale, Scoville and Sage hunkered down in the shade of the overhang. Scoville got out his pipe.

"You seem to be an observing cuss, Sage. How about giving me a rough layout of the island?"

Sage nodded, smoothed an area of earth beside him with a brushing palm, and then began drawing lines with the end of a match.

"You, of course, know how the big rivers run. Here's the Sacramento, coming down—so. And the San Joaquin heads in from the south, like this. The main waters come together about here and then go on out through the straits to San Francisco Bay and the ocean beyond. All right. Now Middle Island lays about here. It's a pretty much four-sided chunk of land with Spanish Slough on the west, Cross Over Slough on the north, Ten Mile Slough on the east, and Back Slough on the south. Middle Island is a pretty sizable stretch, as delta islands go, runnin' about twelve miles long and eight or nine miles wide."

Dan Scoville nodded. "I got all that pretty well from a map in Frank Ide's office in Riverton. What I want mainly, Sage, is where the different outfits are located."

Sage smoothed the ground again, drew more lines. "This is the island. About central and toward the south end, is the Block L headquarters—Logan headquarters. Farther north and west, about here, is Mal Baine's Circle Cross. Almost straight across from Mal Baine and mebbe a little farther north, is Ward Requa's Arrowhead layout. They're the three main cow outfits on the island. There's a couple of other little fellers like Pod Hunber and Hughy Ladd. But they don't amount to shucks. And they won't be concerned in any pullin' and haulin' you might run across."

Scoville swung his head, his eyes sharpening. "Pulling and hauling? You mean between the big three cow outfits?"

Sage spat in disgust. "There I go," he grumbled. "Lettin' my big mouth run away with me. Suppose we just forget I said anything."

Scoville dropped a hand on Sage's arm. "You know damned well I'm not going around yelling anything you tell me at the top of my lungs. But I'm trying to get a fair picture; and the fairer it is, the fairer I'll be able to handle everybody."

"Um!" grunted Sage. "Mebbe you're right. After all, I guess it's no secret that Ward Requa and Cole Logan don't get along too well. Mal Baine—well, he sits pretty well clear, though if he had to take sides, it'd be with Logan. I guess it's too much to expect of human nature that everybody get along all the time."

Ed Jethro came out with the bill of sale, and Scoville paid him for the horse. As Scoville pocketed the bill of sale, the two cowhands came jogging downstreet from the store, saddle gear creaking rhythmically. They nodded to Sage and

Ed Jethro as they passed, and then, when just about to swing off the street into the main island road, reined in to pass a word or two with a third rider just coming into town.

Sage's bleached brows pulled down a trifle as he glimpsed the new arrival. "Rack Logan," he murmured softly. "Streak of mean devil in this fellow, Scoville. Good one to stay away from."

Dan Scoville, recalling that Ward Requa had indicated the same opinion of Rack Logan, studied the fellow as he pulled away from the two Circle Cross hands and came on along the street. Under the pulled-down brim of Rack Logan's hat, Scoville saw the outline of a narrow face, pale eyes, and a thin, harsh line of a mouth. There was a cold and studied insolence in those pale eyes as they touched the group of three in front of the stable and centered on Dan Scoville.

Rack Logan neither spoke nor showed any sign of recognition, but as he came even he deliberately spat into the dust. Then he went on, truculence in the high lift of his shoulders. He turned in at the Wagon Wheel Saloon up street.

"Proud hombre, wasn't he?" drawled Scoville.

"Wrong word," twanged Ed Jethro. "Mean is a better one. Mean as hell!"

Sage darted a quick look at Jethro. "Saying that right here is all right, Ed. But I wouldn't spread it too far."

"I ain't trying to spread nothin'," retorted

the little stable owner sturdily. "Neither am I backin' away from an honest opinion that you and everybody else knows is right, Sage. Big difference between Rack and Cole Logan. Cole's a tough hombre, all right. But he's not mean and he's square. But Rack—" Jethro finished with a shrug.

Dan Scoville straightened up. "Don't shy away from my new office, friends. Drop in any time and make yourselves at home. I like company."

He went off, angling toward the store. Sage watched him for a moment, then turned to Jethro. "Well, what do you think?"

"I like him," said Jethro flatly. "Walks and talks and acts like a man. And well damn able to take care of himself in any company, I'd say. Going to be some changes in these parts, Sage."

Sage nodded slowly. "I think so. Yet, all in all, Ed—Cole Logan hasn't done such a bad job."

"No, he hasn't," conceded Jethro. "Most people realize that. Which is why they been content to let him handle things on the island. They'd have rose up against him long ago, otherwise. But it couldn't last forever. Time was bound to come when somebody like Dan Scoville was sent in to take over. Now that it has, I sure hope Cole is smart enough to read the facts right and act accordingly. Yeah, I sure hope so."

Sage sighed deeply. "So do I. But I'm afraid it ain't going to be that simple. Scoville and

Cole have already butted chins, and Cole came off second best. That ain't goin' to set well, for Cole's a proud man. About all fellers like you and me can do is sit back and hope."

IV—Heavy Fists

It was good to be in the saddle again, with a sound horse under him. For the claybank gelding was a sound horse, easy-gaited, with just the right amount of spirit in it. Riding along the levee top, into the eye of the rising sun, Dan Scoville reflected that he'd gotten a real bargain from Ed Jethro in the gelding.

The afternoon and evening of the day before, his first in Delta, had been quiet and uneventful. After leaving Sage and Ed Jethro at the stable, Scoville had stayed pretty close to his office. Through the open door, around midafternoon, he'd seen Rack Logan ride out of town again, had caught the turn of the man's narrow head, and seen his pale-eyed glance searching that side of the street. But Rack did not pause, and his horse was galloping by the time he cleared the limits of town.

It was a certainty, Scoville realized, that by this time the word of his arrival in Delta had been well circulated across the island, and that many men would be curious to see him and measure him. And right then he'd decided that, instead of waiting for them to come to him, he'd go to them. He'd ride Middle Island, meet its people in quiet friendliness, and let them all see that the law was there to keep a good balance for all and to play no favors.

So he had turned in for the night early, had a good sleep, and was now out to meet the morning and what it might hold.

The way along the levee top was more of a trail than a road. Cross Over Slough ran at his left, steaming a little with mists at this early hour. At intervals, Scoville passed shanties clinging to the slough side of the levee, with an occasional shanty boat nudging the bank, mooring ropes sagging and slime-coated. Wisps of pale wood smoke curled from rusty chimneys and the odors of cooking mingled with the dank, over-all breath of the slough waters.

A few humans were in evidence, several men, a slattern woman or two, and at one cabin a pair of towheaded, ragged kids watched him ride by in big-eyed silence. A certain furtiveness, tinged with belligerence, was reflected by most of the men; it was as though they disliked and were suspicious of any man in the saddle, stranger or not.

At one place a couple of mongrel dogs yapped at the heels of the gelding and, farther along, Scoville came face to face with a lank, gangling fellow who carried a rusty double-barreled shotgun across one arm and a brace of brush rabbits in his other hand. The fellow stepped off the trail to let Scoville pass, but he said nothing and gave no answering sign to Scoville's nod.

To Scoville's right the island was a wide land, heavily grassed, the all-over impression that of a plainlike flatness which buried its far distances in the blur of morning's haze. Out there, looking small against the earth across the width of a couple of miles, were a group of buildings, a windmill tower lifting above them, the mill itself glinting in the climbing sun. Scoville reined the gelding down from the levee top and headed that way.

Coming closer to the ranch, he began passing cattle carrying an Arrowhead iron and, when he rode up past a spread of corrals, it was Ward Requa who stood in the doorway of one of the buildings and raised a casual arm in salute.

"A surprise, and a welcome one," said Requa. "Light down, friend, and help me empty the coffeepot."

A couple of riders were saddling up at one of the corrals, and Requa called across to them, "You boys go ahead with that chore. I'll be out later."

"Don't let me keep you from your honest work," said Scoville, as he stepped from his saddle. "I got nothing on my mind but my hat. I'm just riding to get an idea of the lay of the land."

Requa grinned. "Think nothing of it. This way, Jake and Stony will have the job about done by the time I get there. Besides, I never could get excited about pushing on a shovel handle, and that's what this chore calls for. Cleaning out some ditches to drain a low chunk of my range. That's one thing about running cattle on a delta island—there's no shortage of water. Too damn much of it, most of the time."

Scoville jerked his head. "Yet you use a windmill."

"Have to get decent drinking water for man and beast," explained Requa. "All the ditch water is brackish—seepage from the sloughs. But you dig a hole in the right spot and you come up with pretty fair drinking water."

Requa led the way inside, filled a heavy cup with steaming coffee, and shoved it across a table to Scoville, then filled one for himself and pulled up a chair. This, Scoville saw at a glance, was a bachelor spread, containing the necessities, but with no frills of any kind. Requa, reading Scoville's thought, showed his twisted grin again.

"That's right. Just Jake and Stony and me. We manage to struggle along. Any new excitement in town?"

"If there was, I missed it," said Scoville dryly. "Any reason why there should be?"

"Yeah—you. Don't get the idea that Cole Logan is through with you, friend. He's not. In front of the whole town you pinned his ears back, yesterday morning. Worse, you did it in front of Nora Baine. If you think Logan is going to forget that in a hurry, you couldn't make a worse mistake."

Scoville looked across the edge of his coffee cup at Requa. "I gather you don't like Cole Logan?"

"You gather right," said Requa flatly. "It works both ways. I don't like him, he don't like me. And if you're wondering how we happen to be able to live on the same island, it's like this. We had our little showdown some time ago, Logan and me. I let it be known in terms he couldn't mistake that his God-and-Cole-Logan idea didn't fool me or scare me a bit. I told him to his teeth that if he ever tried to ride my hump I'd throw a gun on him and make it stick. He must have believed me, for he's ridden around me pretty carefully ever since."

"In that case," said Scoville shrewdly, "I wouldn't think you'd be too concerned one way or the other about me setting up an office in Delta. Yet you seemed glad I showed up."

"Glad!" exclaimed Requa. "Hell, man—of course I am. It's bound to clear the air, and that's what I want to see. Think I like to ride around with a gun on my hip all the time? I don't. That's a hell of a way for neighbors to act. But up until now it was the only way a man could feel safe."

"Didn't know things were quite that bad on Middle Island," observed Scoville.

Ward Requa waved a scoffing hand. "You don't

realize the half of it, Scoville. These sloughs, these backwaters, they hide plenty of secrets. Men disappear. One day you see 'em, then you never see them again. Once in a while one is found floating. Like Jack Neely was—with a rope still around his neck and a bullet hole in him."

"Heard about that," said Scoville briefly. "That sort of thing isn't good—not good at all." He pushed back his chair, rummaged for his pipe, his face grave and noncommittal. "Which way to Mal Baine's outfit?"

"Almost due west," said Requa, spinning up a cigarette. "Take my road out to the main island road, then head south a bit. First turn off to the right will take you to Circle Cross."

"What sort is Baine?"

Requa shrugged. "Good enough. Leans some to being the tail to Cole Logan's kite. Maybe he's smart, for that's the safest way to keep Logan off your neck. Yet, to do it, a man would have to give away some of his self-respect."

They went out into the morning sunshine again, and Scoville climbed into his saddle.

"Good-looking bronc you're riding," observed Ward Requa.

Scoville nodded. "Ed Jethro said it was a good one when he sold it to me. He wasn't lying."

"Only one thing lacking," Requa said. "You should have a rifle under your leg."

Scoville looked at him keenly. "How's that?"

"Flat country," said Requa. "And a six-shooter ain't much for range. You might never need a rifle, but then again you might."

Scoville shook his head. "I can't believe things are that bad."

Requa tipped a shoulder in his enigmatic way. "Hope you're right. Drop by any time."

Scoville reined the claybank gelding away, saying over his shoulder, "Thanks for the coffee."

The road from the Arrowhead ran a straight line out into the heart of the island. Here and there across this land wound narrow reed- and tule-banked ditches, and several times when the gelding's jogging hoofs rang hollow echoes on small, planked bridges that crossed these, some wild duck bounced into flight, or the splatter and splash of the clumsier and less agile mud hen made a floundering along the ditch waters.

Cattle grazed beside the road, for some time all of them showing Ward Requa's Arrowhead brand. But as Scoville cut down the distance and came closer to the main island road, he began seeing an occasional critter wearing Mal Baine's Circle Cross and presently, here and there, Cole Logan's Block L showed. The feed was lush, the cattle fat.

A hundred yards back from the road, from the loft of its weathered tower, a windmill spun and clanked to the push of a warming breeze and a pipe poured water into a long and dripping trough where several cattle were drinking. When he swung his head, Dan Scoville could pick up the spinning glint of other windmills across the reaching distances. Here, he mused, was a wonderful setup for cattle. Fat range, plenty of water, and with the far-running miles fenced naturally all about by slough and levee.

In time he reached the main island road and turned the gelding south along it, looking for the turnoff that would take him to Mal Baine's Circle Cross headquarters. Dust winnowed up on the main road ahead of him, and some of the same amber haze coiled up ahead and to his right. Watching with casual interest, Scoville saw riders grow and take shape in both places. Two riders in front of him, a large group to his right. Meaning what, if anything? His eyes narrowed and sharpened.

The two coming in ahead of him were the closer to him, and presently Scoville saw that one of these was a girl. And with a small, startling jolt, he recognized her companion as being the man whom Sage and Ed Jethro had identified as being Rack Logan, yesterday afternoon in town. He of the narrow face and head, the pale eyes and the harsh slit of a mouth. He stared at Scoville with unwinking intensity.

But it was the girl who made Dan Scoville catch a quick breath. He'd seen pretty girls before, lots of them, but where their beauty left off, this girl's began. Part of it was in the obvious pride of her, part in physical perfections. But mainly it was something more, a certain vividness of spirit.

Her hat, pushed slightly back, cupped soft, dark hair about her temples, and her gray eyes were faultlessly clear and steady. Her riding garb was simple enough, yet obviously of the finest materials. Her saddle was no ordinary one, but a masterpiece of hand-stamped leather and silver mountings. Her horse was a glossy black, curried and brushed to the last inch, and showing the fire of warm blood in the way it kept fretting at the snaffle.

Dan Scoville wondered how much of this girl's startling beauty was her own, and how much was contrast with the harsh savagery in the look and manner of the man riding with her.

Scoville pulled well off to his side of the road, his glance holding on the girl. Perhaps he gave the impression of crass staring, though he did not mean it that way. At any rate, Rack Logan, his bitter lips pulling into a sudden twist, started to rein right at Scoville.

The girl spoke a single curt word. "Rack!"

Then she rode on past, and Rack, his cold eyes frankly hating, swung his horse away and followed her.

Scoville, pulling the gelding to a walk, went slowly on, shaking his head a little, like a man dazed. The impulsc to turn and follow the girl with his eyes was almost overpowering. He shook his head again. What the devil was the matter with him?

Yeah, he'd seen pretty girls before—plenty of them. Maybe none like this one—but what of it? He was a man grown, not some bug-eyed kid. He pulled to a halt, bemused, a little bewildered and astounded with himself.

That fellow riding with her—Rack Logan! When or where had he ever seen a tougher-looking hombre? Or one with an expression more coldly malignant? Beauty and the beast, for sure. Damndest combination he'd ever run across. His senses seemed clogged with a fog of unreality.

He was fumbling for his pipe when Duff Twining's voice cut harshly through his mixed-up absorption.

"Acts likc he was heat-struck. Wake up, law man!"

There were four of them and they made up the group approaching from the right, and Dan Scoville, lost in the turmoil of his thoughts, had forgotten them and paid no attention to their swift advance. Until now . . .

Four of them. Duff Twining and Waco Dart. Cole Logan. And an older man, solid and square in his saddle, but with eyes that the years had faded and puckered and made a little weary, as was the mouth that was half hidden by a ragged and grizzled mustache.

Dan Scoville's glance ran over them swiftly, then came back to the guns which Duff Twining and Waco Dart held on him. They had him bracketed, Twining ahead and a little to one side, Waco Dart at the same angle behind him.

"This time," said Duff Twining, "it's different. Put your hands on that saddle horn and keep them there. Now!"

There was nothing else to do but obey. To try for his gun now would be sheer lunacy, for he was between a cross fire that could lift him out of the saddle. Besides, there was no good reason for forcing the issue that far.

After his first start of surprise, a thin gust of anger swept through Scoville. At himself mainly, for allowing himself to be caught off guard in such ignominious a manner. And all because of a pretty face. But this anger faded out and curiosity touched him. Just what could they intend doing with him? Certainly nothing too severe. He folded his hands on his saddle horn.

"Smart," said Duff Twining. "Keep them there!"

Saddle gear creaked as Waco Dart moved up from the rear and lifted away Scoville's gun. Duff Twining's eyes pinched down in a hard mockery.

"Where's the big, bold star now, law man?"

"Right where it's always been," answered

Scoville evenly. "You're buying trouble for yourselves, you know."

"That," retorted Twining, "we'll see." He shot a glance at Cole Logan and said, with rising inflection, "Waco?"

"No," growled Logan. "This is my chore. All right, Deputy—get off that horse!"

For the first time the older man spoke. "I still say you should go slow, Cole. There's a lot more behind that star than just one man."

"One man is all I can see right now," Logan said harshly. "I'll handle him and I'll handle any others that follow him. You heard me, Scoville—get off that horse!"

While he spoke, Cole Logan was stepping from his own saddle. With a couple of swift jerks he unbuckled the gun belt from about his waist, hung it and the holstered gun on his saddle horn. Then he turned, came ahead a few steps, spread his feet, and flexed his heavy fists.

Again the older man spoke up. "Cole, you're wrong. That man ain't afraid and he won't scare. You ain't dealing with some sniveling shanty-boater that you can put the fear of God into. This is a different setup entirely. I say that—"

"And I don't care a thin damn what you say, Mal," cut in Logan. "You just keep out of this. I know what I'm doing. Scoville, are you getting off that horse or do I have to drag you off?"

Dan Scoville shrugged and swung to the

ground. “Anything to oblige.” He squared around and faced Logan, and jeered mildly, “What’s it to be, burning at the stake?”

Cole Logan paid no attention to this. “I got no patience with fools,” he said solidly. “I tried to give you the general idea back in town yesterday, but apparently it didn’t take. I got no time or patience for mouth argument, either. For when all the talk has been made, there’s still only one way to settle who’s boss. I like that way best because it’s so damn definite. Maybe it’s the hard way, but it works. Now I’m going to show you who’s the real law in these parts. Get your fists up!”

Dan Scoville looked this man up and down. Not with any particular anger, but with some wonder at his mental processes. “You,” he drawled, “sure got some primitive ideas. With your two fists you’d lick this star and all that it stands for? My friend, it’s not that simple.” He jerked his head toward the older man. “You better listen to him. He sees this thing right, and you don’t. You keep on this way and you’re breeding one hell of a scab on your nose. Suppose we come down to earth and talk sense?”

In his guttural voice, Waco Dart said, “Cole, he’s yellow—yellow as hell.”

Cole Logan nodded. “I’m beginning to think so. Well, if that’s his color, I’ll sure bring it all out of him.”

Dan Scoville shrugged, those little lines of

pressure at his lip corners deepening. He spoke with burning, open sarcasm. "How pigheaded can a fool man be!"

Now came further interruption, approaching hoofs thumping up from behind. It was the girl and Rack Logan who had turned back. And the girl's voice rang clearly.

"Cole! What's the idea of this? What are you intending to do?"

Logan looked past Scoville, impatience glinting in his eyes. "Nothing to concern you, Loren—or for you to see. Rack, get her out of here!"

Dan Scoville turned to see this. The girl was standing high and forward-leaning in her stirrups. Her eyes were flashing. Rack, his narrow face set, was shouldering his horse at hers, talking to her in a low, toneless drone. The girl spun her horse clear, lifted her quirt.

"Rack—keep your place!" Her flashing glance came back to Cole Logan. "I'm a Logan, too," she cried. "Now if you're bound to be stupid and brutal, then I've got to stay and share your shame. What have you got against this man?"

Cole Logan swung his head doggedly. "That's between him and me—and I'm tired of talking."

He came at Scoville with an explosive rush. Scoville, tightly strung and alert for anything now, dodged one flailing fist, had another slide off the round of his shoulder. Then he dug his own left into the thick torso in front of him and brought his right up and over in a savage hook.

The punch landed squarely, full on the point of Cole Logan's jaw. And Cole went down and lay there for a moment, staring up at Scoville, blank and unbelieving surprise on his face. Off to one side, Waco Dart spat thick words.

"Let me have him, Cole. I'll take that out of him—quick!"

Cole pulled to his knees, shaking the fog from his head. He shot brittle words at Waco Dart.

"Shut up! You keep out of this, Waco. Everybody keeps out of it but him and me. I can handle things."

He got to his feet. He'd lost his hat and his shaggy mane of hair was awry, some of it falling down across his forehead. Dan Scoville thought of an angry bear, glaring at him.

Scoville knew right then that he was in for it. He'd never hit a man a harder or more perfectly placed punch. It had dropped Cole Logan, but its only real effect apparently was to surprise Cole more than it had hurt him. Yeah, thought Scoville bleakly, this was going to be rough, very rough.

"You won't," growled Cole Logan, "pull that one on me again. Coming at you, Deputy!"

There was more cunning and less headlong recklessness in Cole's charge this time. For, though Scoville's blow had not damaged him too much, it had put him flat on his back, and in that moment Cole knew that in this lean, tight-lipped man he was facing something not to be trifled with too much. So, while Cole came in again, he had his hands high and he was crouching slightly and weaving.

Dan Scoville feinted with a straight left, then tried again for that heavy jaw. But this time the blow was warded off by a thick arm, and then what seemed like a post maul smashed home to the side of his head.

Another force hit him, full length, and dimly he realized that this was the ground. He was down, in the dust, and Cole Logan stood over him, feet spread, big fists swinging back and forth.

"That," growled Cole, "is just the start. Get up!"

Instinct told Scoville to wait a bit, wait until his scrambled wits steadied down a bit, for the world was all a crazy dance about him and a strange, dragging numbness slugged his muscles. But another instinct, that of reflex, had him back on his feet before clearer thought could become effective.

He saw Cole's fist coming again, but he couldn't get out of the way of it. Again the world seemed to explode and again he was down. Dimly, as from some great distance, he heard Waco Dart's exultant yell.

"Boot him, Cole! Kick his ribs in. You got him where you want him now. Boot him!"

And as dimly came Cole Logan's reply. "You're

a mean dog, Waco. Someday I'll knock all that out of you—!"

Then it was as though some invisible wire had snapped, letting in full light and feeling again. Strange, the way a man's coordination could be gone one moment, then back the next. . . . As Scoville hit his feet this time, he was in full control of himself once more. But he wasn't showing this fact to Logan. Instead, he wobbled and weaved, reeling a little as he began to circle his man, arms hanging limply at his sides.

And there was white anger in him now, raw and burning. The rising fever of physical combat, which made a man forget everything but the adversary in front of him, and the need of cutting that adversary down to size. He let his head sag and roll, but through slitted lids his eyes were bleak and cold and watchful.

Cole Logan fell for the ruse. He saw only a man shambling unsteadily about him, seemingly out on his feet. So he moved in confidently, intent on finishing this thing with the next punch. But the blow which came was not his own, for Scoville, suddenly steadying, drove a winging right fist that landed crushingly on Cole's mouth. It staggered Cole, set him back on his heels, and brought a spurt of crimson that ran down Cole's chin and smeared the front of his shirt.

"Friend," said Dan Scoville thinly, "those fists of yours are heavy. But we'll see—we'll see—!"

Cole Logan shook his head, blew the blood from his mashed lips, and came in, berserk and wild. Scoville sighted for his jaw again, but the blow was too high, catching Cole under the eye. The blow was a savage one, but not enough to stop Cole's raging charge. And before Scoville could dodge clear, Cole got hold of him.

This man was bull strong and wild with fury. He literally flung Scoville around and around, and it was all Scoville could do to keep partly on his feet, let alone throw any punches. Then Cole stumbled and they both went down, rolling over and over like a pair of savage dogs.

Scoville had no chance at this sort of business. He was smashed back and forth against the earth, thc wcight and power of Cole Logan beating and pounding on him. His only chance lay in his superior speed and agility, and it was these which enabled him to finally pull clear and lurch to his feet. Under him his legs were trembling and he rocked back and forth.

This was not a calculated ruse, as before. This was the real result of terrific punishment. For those few moments of wild mauling had been worse than any blows. Scoville felt wrenched and disjointed, all through. This fellow Cole Logan, like a grizzly bear, had it in him to fairly crush the life out of a man. And now, as Cole came lunging up and at him again, Scoville gave back and back, trying desperately to drag new strength into himself once more.

The girl was crying, "Cole, stop it—stop it! Cole—!"

But neither of them heard her. They circled each other, bloody and disheveled. And, even if he had heard his sister's cry, Cole would have paid it no heed. For he wasn't stopping anything. He came in remorselessly, peering up at Scoville from under that matted tangle of hair.

Scoville set himself and smashed out with both fists. They landed, but they did not stop this juggernaut of a man in front of him. Fists came back at him, crushing, lethal with hurt. They clubbed into his face, his body, the side of his neck. And he was down again. . . .

He didn't remember getting up, or how. But his fist went into Cole Logan's face once more, the wild shock of the punch running clear up to his shoulder. It was like hitting a wall—a bloody wall.

Thunder and hell exploded in his own head once more, and now he was face down in the dust and when he tried to drag air into his starved lungs, dust stung his nostrils and choked his throat. He rolled his head, got his hands under him and pushed slowly up, a man no longer fully conscious of his own movements. Only, 'way back somewhere in his being, there was something exhorting him to get up—get up!

They watched him, Duff Twining—the older man, Mal—and Waco Dart. They watched him with something like awe in their eyes. Watched him go down and get up, go down and get up. Watched him, even as he reeled around, set Cole Logan back on his heels with another wicked smash to Cole's beaten mouth.

"Law man he might be," muttered Duff Twining once. "But by God he's all man—all man!"

There were two others watching, also. The girl on the black horse, no longer crying at Cole Logan to stop it, for she knew now that such protest was useless. Instead she wept, strange weeping which left her face frozen of expression, but with tears running down her face. But Rack, he of the baleful, pale, malevolent eyes, missed not a single blow as he followed it all with an absorbed, avid ferocity.

Dan Scoville was completely unaware of any of this. For he was out on his feet, his eyes glazed, his senses gone. He reeled around, completely helpless. Cole Logan, following, his right fist cocked for another wicked smash, stopped, shook his head, and dropped that poised fist by his side.

"Can't do it," he blurted thickly to himself. "No heart to hit that man again—"

And then, suddenly, Dan Scoville was down again. Cole Logan hadn't hit him, hadn't touched him. It was just that there was a limit to how far the indomitable spirit could carry the wavering flesh, and Dan Scoville had passed that limit. His knees simply caved, he toppled on his face, rolled over and lay still, drowned in the blackness of complete insensibility.

Cole Logan, beginning to stagger himself, found his horse beside him. He caught at the saddle with both hands, leaned there, shaggy head dropping forward to rest on one arm. And the girl, swinging her black that way, lashed at Cole with furious words.

"Cole—what kind of a brute are you—?"

Then she was swiftly out of the saddle and over beside Dan Scoville, dropping on her knees beside him. Seeing this, Rack Logan cursed, lifting his horse ahead.

"Loren—get up out of there! You fool girl—get back in your saddle!"

Cole Logan lifted his head, came around, his voice thick and heavy with exhaustion. "Shut up, Rack! Don't you use that tone on Loren. Keep out of this!"

There was a canteen slung to Cole's saddle. He fumbled at this, got it loose, then, steadier on his feet, moved over to Dan Scoville. He tipped the canteen, sloshed a gout of water across Scoville's face. He spoke to the girl, a softening note in his voice.

"You shouldn't have ridden back, Loren. I wouldn't have you see such things."

"But I did," she cried. "I saw it all. Did you have to beat him—and beat him—?"

"Yeah," said Cole heavily. "I did. Else he'd have torn my head off. I walked into something with this fellow, and had to finish it." He paused, his heavy jaw stealing out while a settled grimness took some of the swollen pout from his bloody lips. "Besides, I'm the law on this island and I had to prove it. So I did!"

He spilled more water on Dan Scoville's face.

Consciousness came back. At first nothing was real except a drained weariness against a background of deep, sodden pain. Then things began to clear, and Dan Scoville knew where he was and what had happened. The girl was on one side of him, dabbing at his face with a water-soaked handkerchief. On the other side was the heavy-shouldered bulk of Cole Logan, the man who had beaten him down to this place in the dust. Between puffed and blackening lids there was respect in Logan's eyes, and now, as Scoville stirred, a certain relief.

"How you feeling?" Logan growled.

"Like I'd been mauled by a grizzly," Scoville mumbled. "But I think I'll live." He rolled his head, looked at the girl. "Thanks. This almost makes the licking worthwhile."

Big-eyed, she stared at him for a moment, a flush touching her face. Then she straightened up and moved away. Cole Logan, going quickly harsh and distant again, took hold of Scoville's shoulder and hauled him to his feet. Logan called, "Duff, bring his horse!"

This Duff Twining did, scooping up Scoville's hat on the way, whipping the dust from it. Scoville spread his feet, put his back against the gelding's shoulder for support. He needed that support, plenty! He pulled his hat low over his eyes, stood that way for a little time, hauling breath into his aching lungs, waiting for the buttery weakness in his legs to subside. He fumbled for his pipe and tobacco pouch, but his hands were stiff and clumsy and swollen and when he tried to fill the pipe he spilled more tobacco than he gained. Harsh-faced Duff Twining, watching with inscrutable eyes, produced tobacco and papers, built a swift cigarette, tucked it into Scoville's lips, and held a match. Scoville inhaled deeply and nodded.

"Thanks."

Then he let his head swing, his glance touching all of them. The girl, standing beside her black horse. Rack, the malevolent one, Waco Dart, and the older man, Mal. And finally Cole Logan, solid and dominant against the sun.

"Well," said Scoville slowly, "you figure you've proven anything, Logan—outside the fact that man to man you just gave me a high-class beating?"

There was an implacable stubbornness in the

cast of Cole Logan's head. "You're going back to town," he said, with rough emphasis. "Then you'll pack your gear and head out for Riverton. When you get there, you can tell Frank Ide that we don't need any outside law on this island. That we can handle our own affairs, that we always have and always will. That's it, Deputy."

Dan Scoville stood silent for a moment, head tipped as he stared at the ground, the pale blue smoke of his cigarette curling up about his beaten face. Things were still a little blurred for him, and he'd have liked nothing better than to slide down to earth again and rest. But he couldn't afford to show any weakness in front of these people. He shook his head slightly, unable to understand this big, dominant man in front of him. Then he turned and, with teeth gritted against the effort, pulled himself into his saddle with slow and painful care.

"Give him back his gun, Waco," ordered Cole Logan.

Scoville took the weapon, dropped it into the holster. He laid his fogged glance on Cole Logan again.

"I'm going back to town, Logan. But no farther. I'll be seeing you again, for I'll be around." He touched the star on his shirt. "Still there, you notice. It'll always be there. If not on me, then on somebody else. You could beat me to death, but you can't beat that star. Use your head, man!

You're big, but you'll never stand tall enough to whip that star and what it stands for."

He looked around at the silent group once more, his glance reaching the girl last and resting there longest. He touched his hat to her. Then he twitched the reins and the claybank moved off, back along the road to Delta. And as they watched him go, they never guessed the terrific effort it took on his part to sit straight-backed in the saddle, or knew that his teeth were clenched and that the cold sweat of an all-over-beaten sickness coursed down his face.

Mal, the older one, broke the silence. "Again I say that was the wrong move, Cole. You didn't prove a thing. Oh, sure—you beat the senses out of him. I never saw a man take a more savage beating. But you didn't whip him. Nobody will ever really whip that man. You might kill him, but you'll never whip him."

Rack, the malevolent one, spoke harshly. "Well, maybe that could happen, too. He's mortal, ain't he?"

Cole Logan swung his head savagely. "Drop that kind of talk, Rack! You're always too damn ready to go wild on the trigger. So, drop it. For the rest of it, I'll still handle things in my own way. Now we get on home—all of us!"

They moved off, the girl the last to put her horse to movement. For a little time she paused, her eyes on that straight-backed figure jogging down the road to town. And Rack, watching her as she watched Dan Scoville, showed the vicious twist about his lips again, while his pale, hooded eyes burned with sullen fire.

With distance and dust behind him, Dan Scoville no longer sat straight-backed in his saddle. Instead, he rode humped 'way over, both hands locked around his saddle horn. He was dizzy and sick with nausea. His head was a thundering torment and his stomach was turning over and over. The muscles on the insides of his thighs were crawling and twitching, and he clamped the saddle doggedly, trying to still them.

He thought that town would never lift out of the sun haze ahead, but it did, finally. The claybank would have turned in at the livery barn, but Scoville reined it along to the tie rail in front of Bill Profitt's store. He slid slowly from the saddle, holding to a stirrup leather to keep from falling down. He didn't dare try and duck under the hitch rail, for he knew if he did he'd pitch forward on his face. So he went all the way along the rail to circle the far end, sliding a hand along the rail to steady himself.

It was an equally long journey, covering the length of the porch to his office door, always with a hand against the store front. Like, he thought with bitter humor, a drunken man feeling his way through a deep alcoholic daze. But he got to the office and into the rear room finally, and over to his bunk. He sagged down on this and flattened out and closed his eyes and let go of everything with a long, broken sigh. And the world ran away from him. . . .

Later, it was barefoot Tod Neely who came along and, wondering about the claybank, looked in and finally stole to the rear room. The startled lad stared down at this blood- and dust-smeared man with the swollen, bruise-blackened face, at the stern mouth unconsciously drawn with pain and drained vitality. Then Tod scurried out and along the porch and into the store.

"Missis Profitt!" he called shrilly. "Missis Profitt!"

V—Affairs of Men

Molly Profitt stood with her hands on her hips, her favorite posture when reflecting deep emphasis or indignation. "I declare if I don't believe I'm beginning to hate Cole Logan!"

Dan Scoville grinned up at her crookedly. "Now don't you, ma'am. Leastways, not on my account."

"But look at you! You're a solid mass of black and blue. That man's a complete brute!"

Scoville showed his crooked grin again. "I wouldn't say that. Oh, it was a pretty rugged go, all right. Couple of times there I figured I must be tangled with a mad bull. But probably right now he's not feeling any too chipper himself. I got me a bite or two while he was collecting himself a meal."

"You take it pretty good," said Molly Profitt. "Better than a lot of men would."

"No use getting too worked up about it," philosophized Scoville. "You get in a ruckus. Somebody gets licked. If it happens to be you, why that's all there is to it. Staying mad doesn't get you anywhere, and you don't heal up any quicker."

"Does this mean that you're through here?"

"No," said Dan Scoville softly. "It means that I'm just starting."

Tod Neely came pattering in, carrying a bucket of steaming water. His boyish face was set in soberness and he looked at Scoville a little diffidently. Knowing what was in the boy's mind, Scoville smiled at him.

"Never was a man so tough, Tod, that he couldn't bump into a tougher one somewhere along the line."

Scoville was stripped to the waist, and over his short ribs a towel, once hot, but now cooling, laid its moist touch. Molly Profitt took this, dipped it into the fresh bucket of hot water, wrung it out, and spread it again on Scoville's bruised midriff.

"I don't believe anything is broken," she observed critically. "But I never saw such a bruise before. He must have used his boots on you."

Scoville, cringing a little under the scalding but soothing touch of the compress, shook his head. "No. The man fought fair. He didn't have to use his boots. His fists were plenty."

"You were alone? Just the two of you, I mean?"

Scoville shook his head again. "Duff Twining was there, and Waco Dart. And an older man. I heard Logan call him Mal."

"Mal Baine, Nora's father. He and Cole Logan get along pretty well. He's a pretty decent sort, Mal Baine is. I'd have thought he'd have stopped this thing."

"He did sort of argue against it," admitted

Scoville. "But Logan was calling the dance, and that was that."

There was a moment of silence, then Scoville said, "Rack Logan was there, too. And a girl. Pretty? Lordy! She rode a black horse and what a picture she made. I gathered that she didn't enjoy the show. Toward the last I wasn't seeing or hearing too good, but a couple of times there I thought I heard her giving Logan fits."

"His sister, Loren," said Molly Profitt. "The darling of the Logan clan. Pretty—yes. But sheltered too much. They guard the poor girl like she was some fragile flower. Of course, Rack would be there, where Loren was. For Rack is the official watchdog. Wherever Loren rides, there you'll find Rack Logan. And if any mere man so much as looks at Loren, let alone speaks to her, then Rack shows his best snarl and wants to make an issue of it, right on the spot. He was all set to use his quirt on George Delbert one day just because George tipped his hat to Loren and remarked that it was a fine day. He would have used the quirt, too, if my Bill hadn't warned him off. I'm sorry for the girl, I really am. She's entitled to a normal existence, but they won't let her lead one."

Scoville stirred a little. "That's kind of hard to understand. What's the reason for it?"

Molly Profitt shrugged her plump shoulders. "Cole's idea mainly, I imagine. Certainly not

Loren's. Oh, she's got her share of the Logan pride, but times when I've talked to her in the store I've sensed that she's full of revolt against the kind of life she's had to live. I've seen her look at her cousin Rack with something almost like hate in her eyes."

"That's not too hard to understand," murmured Scoville. "I think I could hate that hombre myself. But why should they have Rack riding herd on the girl? This island ain't that wild."

"Of course it isn't," declared Molly Profitt. "Oh, we've some shady characters, all right, hanging out in some of the cabins and shanty boats along the sloughs—but none that shady. Like I said, it's probably all Cole Logan's idea—and for effect, more than anything else. No question that Cole is very fond of his sister, and he'd naturally want to guard her against anything unpleasant. But I think it feeds his black, wild pride to set her up as something sort of extra special, something sort of emblematic of Logan position and power. Whatever it is, it's not being very fair to Loren."

She took the compress off Scoville's ribs, dipped it in the hot water, wrung it out, and replaced it.

"How long you aiming to dab these towels on me, ma'am?" queried Scoville.

"Just as long as I figure them necessary," Molly Profitt told him firmly. "So you might just as well quit squirming and wriggling. You're not going anywhere except to sleep when I'm finished with you."

It was coming on sundown when he awoke. He was alone and the room was very still. A light blanket was over him. He pushed this aside, swung his feet off the bunk, and sat up, his teeth set against the protest of tortured, stiffened muscles. It was as though he'd been beaten all over with clubs. But his head was clear and the gleam of renewed vitality was in his eyes.

He got to his feet and moved slowly up and down the room, rolling his shoulders and swinging his arms to loosen up. His shirt, freshly washed and dried and ironed, hung at the head of the bunk. His eyes softened as he slowly and carefully donned this.

Molly Profitt! It was big-souled, warm-hearted women like her who kept the world of men from becoming a jungle. . . .

He found his pipe, loaded and lighted it, moved out into the main office and to the door, where he stood, looking up and down the street. A couple of men came out of the store, one of them carrying a dirty flour sack, the bottom of which sagged and bulged with a few purchases of some sort. They felt his glance and returned it, a certain sardonic skepticism showing. There was a shiftless, careless look about them, and Scoville catalogued them as a pair of shanty-boat or levee cabin men. They moved off along the porch at a dragging shuffle, the mutter of their voices carrying back to him, and he caught one spoken comment clearly.

"Guess we heard right. Logan sure worked him over. He won't last."

Irritation nagged at Scoville, his eyes darkened and his lip corners thinned. The star as a front isn't going to be enough, he thought bleakly. Somewhere along the line they're going to have to be shown there's a man behind it.

The ruffle of hoofs downstreet turned his attention that way. It was Ward Requa riding in. Requa was heading straight for the office, so Scoville turned back in and was slouched in his chair when Requa came in, that small, cynical smile lurking at his lips.

"The word got around, Scoville. Thought I'd take a ride and a look at the casualty. You seem fairly healthy."

"I think so," said Scoville dryly. "Have a chair."

Requa sat down, located a stogie in a pocket, lit it, and puffed reflectively. "Took less time than I thought it would," he observed. "For you to get some of the answers, I mean. Where does it leave you?"

"Right where you see me. I'm staying, if that's what you're driving at."

Requa blew a thin line of smoke at the ceiling. "Cole Logan will be figuring otherwise. I know how the man's mind works. If there's anybody around that you want to get rid of, why then you go over him, rough! Put the fear of God in him so he'll run and keep on running. It works, generally, so Logan sticks pretty close to the idea."

"And when it doesn't work?" suggested Scoville.

Requa shrugged. "Then it's like I told you this morning. The trail gets really rocky. Somebody finds a dead man, lying out along some trail, or hanging to a tree on the levee, or floating in a slough. For, you see, as a last resort there's always cousin Rack to fall back on. Wait until you meet up with cousin Rack, friend. Then you'll see what I mean."

"I've seen him," said Scoville. "He was there. Got to admit he looked the part, all right."

"Rack Logan," said Requa deliberately, "would pull the legs off a frog, just to watch it die. That man's a wolf that's learned to walk on its hind legs."

Dan Scoville laid a sharply probing glance at this man across the table from him. "You sure got definite ideas about the Logans. None of them complimentary. I can't figure how you've managed to stay on the same island with them."

That cynical smile still hovered on Requa's lips, but now his eyes showed a sudden cold glint.

"I told you why, this morning. I pack a gun. So do a couple of pretty good men I got riding for me. Logan knows why we pack 'em. It's a language he understands, and the only one. But I say again, that's a hell of a way for men to have to live. Me, I yearn to be able to ride my range without watching every ditch and levee and tule clump, wondering all the time which one might hold somebody with a rifle trained on me."

"I can understand that," nodded Scoville, his eyes narrowed and musing. "Well, Cole Logan may figure he's won something. But he hasn't. Oh, he whipped me to a fare-ye-well, all right. I sure absorbed a high-class going over. But the star is still here, and it'll stay!"

"It'll stay," said Requa bluntly, "only if you put enough weight behind it. By that I mean you'll have to take off the gloves—take them really off. Rough ones only understand the same sort of thing that they hand out—but more so. You'll see I'm right."

Requa got up, moved to the door, paused there, his grin showing again over his shoulder. "If you figure raw meat will do that left eye of yours any good, I'll be glad to slaughter a critter and bring you a supply."

"Thanks. But Molly Profitt's done pretty well on it with her own kind of remedy."

"Now," said Requa, with emphasis, "there is one grand woman! You've been in good hands."

Scoville sat for some little time in thought after Requa had gone. By the time he got up and left his office, walking slowly, the sun was down and taking over was the dusk, its blue mists running far and cool. At the stage road turnoff, Scoville climbed the slope of the levee and saw Tod Neely squatting on the end of the wharf, fishline dangling. He moved over beside the boy.

"Mind if I watch, Tod?"

"Shucks, of course not!" exclaimed the boy. "You want, I'll round up another line for you. Fishin' can get good at this time of day."

Scoville shook his head. "I'll just watch you catch 'em."

To Dan Scoville, this twilight hour had always been the loneliest time of the day, no matter what part of the land he might be standing on at the moment. A kind of good loneliness, when a man could rest. Here it seemed especially so. Space, empty horizons, evening mists climbing. Brown waters of Cross Over Slough slowly stirring under the shift of the tide, the influence of a restless ocean near a hundred miles distant.

In the far distance a duck quacked, once. A wisp of shore birds ruffed past, on the way to some destination for the night. A bittern, awkward and homely even in flight, winged across the sky's fading sunset glow, and its croaking was a solitary, empty sound against the world's great silence.

Only his soreness and stiffness served to remind Dan Scoville that this day had held all that it had. At any rate, here for a time was peace. And the chance to think of a girl with wide, gray eyes and a beauty so startling it struck a man like a club.

Scoville's thoughts were cut through by an abrupt question from the boy beside him. "How come you let Cole Logan lick you, Dan?"

Startled, he stared down at the boy. Tod was not looking at him, seemed to have all his attention focused on his fishline. Scoville smiled slightly. He knew how this lad's thoughts were running. Boylike, Tod had known the beginnings of hero worship, and the ideal had been knocked into a cocked hat because his hero had come off second best in a brawl. Scoville answered quietly.

"The only man who never takes a whipping, Tod, is the one who never gets in a fight. No matter how good you are, somewhere you bump into somebody who's better at that sort of thing. Everybody is bound to take some kind of whipping during his life—probably several of them."

Now the boy looked up, a surprising fierceness making his voice shrill. "You got a gun. Why didn't you use it on him?"

"Wasn't that kind of a fight, Tod," explained Scoville. "I'm glad it wasn't. Gun fights are always bad business, no matter who wins. And Cole Logan fought fair, Tod."

“He didn’t fight fair when he killed my pap,” charged the boy doggedly.

Scoville dropped a hand on the boy’s shoulder. “Now you’re not fighting fair, Tod. For you don’t know for sure that Cole Logan had anything to do with the death of your father. And it’s not fair to say that he did, unless you’re absolutely sure. Lots of people get charged with things they’re not guilty of. It could be that way with Cole Logan.”

The boy digested this for a moment before muttering, “Sure seems funny to me that you’d stand up for Cole Logan, after him givin’ you such a beating.”

“Sometimes,” went on Scoville patiently, “a fight produces queer things, Tod. Plenty of times you find out more about the other fellow in a fight with him than you’d ever learn otherwise. For when a man is blind mad in the heat of a fight, if there’s an extra mean, crooked streak in him, that’s when it will show up. In a fight you can learn to despise the other fellow, or learn to respect him, depending how he acts. Once, when I was about your age, another boy and me had quite a go. Looking back, considering our ages at the time, I think it was about as tough a brawl as I ever got into. I forget who won. That didn’t matter. What counted was that after the fight, the other boy and I became fast friends and stayed so. It’s better to come out of a fight that way, Tod, than hating the other fellow forever just because he licked you."

The boy stared up at him, incredulous. "You mean, you aim to be friends with Cole Logan?"

"Maybe. I hope so. I'm remembering he fought fair, Tod. And a man who fights fair generally lives that way, within limits."

While the boy was trying to digest this, a man came out of a shanty boat tied a little way up from the wharf. It was the same fellow who had sat alongside of Scoville in the eating house yesterday noon. A man given over to an excess of soft fat, with a veined, foxy face and a grizzle of dirty gray whiskers on his jowls. He climbed the short slope to the wharf.

"Any luck yet, Tod?" he asked, his voice as meaty as his body.

The boy shook his head. "Not yet, Maze." Then, a little awkwardly, almost apologetically, he added, "This is Dan Scoville, our new law man. Dan, this is Maze Dickson. I live with him."

Scoville gave Dickson a cool, quick survey, nodded. "Howdy!" There was little cordiality in his tone, or in his thoughts, either. For this rum-soaked, slovenly individual was hardly the best sort of companion for a kid like Tod.

"Sure glad you've set up an office in Delta, Mister Scoville," wheezed Dickson. "That's fine—fine! Something this island has been needin' for a long, long time. For it's high time that Cole Logan was put in his place. Yes, sir—damn high time!"

"Just Cole Logan—or some others as well?" asked Scoville curtly.

The fellow's eyes flickered. "There could be others. But Cole Logan is the big he-wolf who needs curryin'. You take care of him and this island will sure be a better place to live on."

Scoville did not answer, using the interval to run another match across the bowl of his pipe. And then came activity at the end of Tod's fishline as a further welcome break. The boy hauled a hefty catfish up onto the planking, where it bounced and slapped about.

"Now there's our supper, Tod!" exclaimed Maze Dickson. "That's a real old lunker. You scatter along to skin and clean it, and I'll be there to put it in the frying pan."

The boy started slowly off, paused at the wharf's edge. "Sometime you want to go fishing, Dan—you let me know. I can get a boat and I'll take you where they really bite."

"That's a deal," nodded Scoville. "One of these days we'll try it, Tod."

The boy trotted along to the shanty boat. With some oiliness, Maze Dickson said, "Now there's a handy kid to have around. Don't know what I'd do without Tod. He's been with me ever since his pap was done in by Cole Logan."

"You sure of that?" Scoville shot the question with such harsh, blunt impact, Dickson's chin sagged a little.

"Su-sure of what?" he blurted.

"That Cole Logan had anything to do with the death of Tod Neely's father? Sure enough to make it a direct charge through proper channels of the law?"

Maze Dickson began to flounder. "Why—uh—well, everybody figures it was Cole Logan who did it."

"Everybody? Who is everybody? Name me some who believe that way."

Maze Dickson named nobody. He said nothing. Dan Scoville stabbed a hard finger into the center of the man's bulging, dirty midriff.

"A word for you and others like you to chew on, Dickson. Murder is a damn tough charge to throw at any man. And unless you can back up your talk with proof, don't make it!"

Scoville turned and walked away into the thickening dusk. Maze Dickson stared after him, foxy face twisting. Dickson cursed softly, spat, and went down to his shanty boat.

Scoville had his supper at Mrs. Tyce's little eating house, then went over to the store, where the lights were on. Bill Profitt was hunched over the counter, figuring in a much-thumbed ledger. He looked up at Scoville's entrance, and his shrewd eyes twinkled slightly. “Well, so far how do you like our island?”

Scoville touched a finger to his sore face. “Got some rough spots on it.” Then he shot a question of his own. “What do you know about this fellow Maze Dickson?”

Bill Profitt straightened, looked at Scoville keenly, as though probing for the real meaning behind the question. He answered slowly, “Nothing in particular, one way or the other. What is there a man like me would know? This delta country is full of fellows like Dickson. They come and they go. They live in shanty boats or levee cabins along this slough or that. Long as they don’t bother me, I pay them little attention.”

“What do they live on?” asked Scoville. “I mean, do they work at anything?”

“Not if they can help it,” was the dry reply. “Mostly, I guess, they live on what they can get out of the slough waters. They get hungry, they catch a fish or two, or maybe shoot a couple of ducks. Some of them trap a little, for mink and coon and skunk, and trade the hides in for flour and stuff like that when Pitch Branner comes by with that rickety old store boat of his. They spend a little money with me, but not enough to make me rich by a hell of a ways. Why you interested in Dickson, especially?”

“Mainly because of Tod Neely. Tod’s a good lad, and I like him. From what he’s told me, he’s had a pretty tough ride of it so far in life, and living under the wing of some shiftless shanty-boater like Dickson doesn't promise much for the kid's future. What I'm leading up to is this. Would you have any objection to me putting up another bunk in my back room for the kid to use?"

Bill Profitt pursed his lips, pulled at them with thumb and forefinger. "Depends," he said succinctly. "You're here now, but how long you going to stay? Suppose you get Tod to bunking with you. Then you pull out. Where does that leave the boy? Right now he's at least got a place to eat and sleep. But you take him away from Dickson, then I doubt Dickson would let him come back, should Tod be left high and dry."

"Suppose we get a couple of things straight, once and for all, Profitt," said Scoville grimly. "Forget this talk of me pulling out. Yeah, I took a walloping from Cole Logan—a real one. That doesn't mean I'm going to run. Right now I'm weighing what I hear, what I see. I aim to keep on doing that until I got facts, instead of talk to go on. The day I do, the day I know exactly the pattern and the stripe of things, then I'll clear the air, damn quick and damn definite. You can believe that!" He paused, then went on with milder tone, "Getting back to Tod Neely—once I start looking after him, I'll keep on looking after him. You can believe that, too."

The storekeeper met the glint in Scoville's eye for a moment, then nodded slowly. "I believe you." He showed a faint smile. "Matter of fact, I've figured you that way from the first. If I hadn't, I'd never have rented to you. About Tod, well, Molly's been after me quite a few times about that kid, saying that he deserved a better show in life. So I know she'll approve of the whole idea. When you figure to take the kid in?"

"That may take a little time. Don't want to rush him. I've already planted the idea. I'd like him to make his own decision. The boy's probably been thinking about it. We'll let things cook a while." Scoville changed the subject. "This town seems quiet enough of nights."

"Early yet," said Bill Profitt. "Most times it's this way, but every now and then it can surprise you." He looked at Scoville keenly again. "So you've had a real go with Cole Logan. Convince you of anything?"

"That he's a tough one with his fists," was Scoville's laconic reply. "Past that, I'm still reserving judgment."

He went out, moved to the edge of the porch. A voice, that of Sage, the stage driver, came softly to him through the dark. "Maybe you're not interested, Dan—but Rack Logan is in town."

Scoville moved toward the voice. Sage was hunkered down by the black doorway of Scoville's office.

"Should I be interested, Sage?" murmured Scoville.

"Was I in your boots, I sure as hell would be," Sage declared. "For you never know what Rack Logan might be up to. He's a mean whelp."

"Where is he now?"

"Saw him go into the Wagon Wheel, just a little ago."

"That's to be expected, isn't it?"

"Mebbe. If he stays there. If—"

Scoville smiled bleakly in the dark. "You think he might come looking for me, Sage?"

Sage pulled to his feet. "You figure it's all a joke, then that makes me a fool," he growled testily. "It's your pie. Cut it any way you want."

Scoville dropped a hand on Sage's shoulder. "Obliged, friend. If Rack's really looking for me, then I mustn't disappoint him."

Sage, mollified, said gruffly, "Watch yourself. I tell you he's a mean one. But don't tell anybody I told you."

Sage slid away into the night, and Scoville stood where he was for a little time, gravely still. He wondered about men like Sage and Bill Profitt. In some ways they seemed to approve of him and his star. In others they fenced themselves with a cautious reserve. They were anxious, yet reluctant. The only answer, as Scoville could see it, was that, despite what they might openly say, deep inside they were afraid he wouldn't last.

And so, if they took his side too openly, they'd be left holding the sack after he had gone.

No doubt their attitude reflected that of most of those here in Delta. They knew that on the day of his arrival he'd faced down Cole Logan, right here in this street. But now they also knew that, man to man, Logan had given him a tough whipping. So they were wary, withholding final judgment.

Which wasn't a good thing. It meant they were skeptical of the star he carried and what it stood for. And he knew he couldn't bring about the results he desired unless everybody was to be shown, once and for all, that neither the star nor the man who carried it was made of such futile stuff.

There was, it seemed, only one way to knock this hesitancy, this doubt, out of them. That was to give them a tough example. Rack Logan was in town. Rack, the malevolent one, whom men seemed to fear even more than they did Cole Logan. At least, they reckoned him more dangerous than Cole. Now, whether Rack had come to town with any idea against the star was only a guess. But if he had, mused Scoville grimly, then he'd have his chance to show his stuff.

Scoville turned into the blackness of his office, well enough acquainted with the layout now to move through it without the aid of a light. He moved into the back room and lifted down his belt and gun, where they had hung on the head of his bunk. He strapped on the weapon, then lifted it from the holster, flipped open the loading gate and spun the cylinder, letting a fingertip run over the head of the cartridges that filled the chambers with their fat deadliness. He dropped the gun back into the holster and went outside again. He paused at the edge of the porch, stretched his arms, drew the night air deep into his lungs, lifted himself on his toes. Then he headed directly along the street toward a spread of lighted window which had the name WAGON WHEEL painted at a slant across the glass.

It was a tawdry little saloon, and with space so taken up with battered card and drinking tables that only an area a couple of yards wide allowed movement up and down in front of the short bar. The place had a stale smell, that of the day's trapped heat, of whiskey dregs and old tobacco smoke.

There were about a dozen men present, more than Dan Scoville had seen in one group since his arrival at Delta. Maze Dickson was one of these, his fat-padded shoulders and foxy face hunched over one of the tables, with three others of the same ilk sitting with him. All had drinks in front of them.

Rack Logan was at the bar, his back to it, leaning there with a boot heel hooked on the brass footrail. He had a whiskey glass in one hand and with the other was emphasizing some droning remark he'd just made. But all talk ceased abruptly when the swinging doors winnowed shut behind Dan Scoville's shoulders. Rack Logan came partly around, to face Scoville more fully.

Scoville had his good look at the whole setup, then moved down along the bar to stop a couple of strides from Rack Logan. He laid his words with blunt abruptness.

"If I was the subject under discussion, don't let my showing up cramp anybody's style."

The silence held and lengthened, and men who had been staring at Dan Scoville now began throwing furtive glances at Rack Logan. Which told Scoville all he wanted to know. He moved a step closer to Rack.

"So my name was being kicked around, eh? Mostly by you, I suppose. Well, whatever it was you were saying, say it again. Now—to my face! Or is that snarly, tough wolf act of yours just an act, with nothing behind it?"

The stillness grew, until it seemed to have positive weight to it. In Rack's pale eyes a crimson spark began to glow. He lifted his glass to his lips, drained it, then came fully around and put the glass on the bar. His harsh words fell tonelessly.

"Yeah, I been talking. I been telling how Cole

beat the everlasting liver out of you. How you are just another two-bit, star-toting four-flusher. How you were going to be kicked off this island unless you damn well got traveling fast enough to haul your own carcass back where it came from. That was the story I was telling. Now have you got any answer to it?"

Rack Logan was cocked for action, cocked and waiting. Dan Scoville could see that, could tell it by the pinpoint spark of crimson in those malevolent eyes, by the cavities of tension at the corners of the thin, bitter lips.

By his words, Rack had laid the issue bare and cold. He had thrown the challenge squarely into Scoville's teeth. It had to be met as ruthlessly as it had been given.

Rack's right side was toward the bar, while the bar was to Dan Scoville's left. There was an advantage in this that Rack did not seem to recognize—and that advantage was with Scoville. Rack found this out in the next few explosive seconds.

"Why, yes," drawled Scoville, almost carelessly, "yes, I got an answer. Like this!"

With the final word, Scoville drove into Rack, hitting him with the point of his left shoulder, putting the turn of his body behind it, and the power in his driving legs. The move slammed Rack into the bar, trapping his right arm momentarily, breaking up the swift grab he made for his gun. And that brief moment of time was all that Scoville needed. With his right hand he whipped out his own gun and cuffed Rack across the side of the head with the solid, heavy flat of the weapon. It was a wicked blow, with cold intent behind it. Rack Logan went down, in a limp, collapsing huddle.

Scoville stepped back. He'd had to establish something in this town and he'd done it in the only way to make it really effective. Now he ran a frosty glance around the startled, breathless room.

"So much for that," he said curtly. "Are there any more doubters?"

If there were, they did not speak up. There was a slight stir, but beyond that only the continued silence. Scoville holstered his gun, leaned over, and lifted away Rack's weapon. He jacked the cartridges from it, then slid the weapon across the bar to the man beyond it, a gangling, bleached individual, thin almost to cadaverousness and with the yellowed skin of a malaria sufferer.

"Keep it for him," ordered Scoville. "Don't give it back to him tonight, though." He turned to the watching room again. "A couple of you drag him out of here, shake some wits back into him, and put him on his horse. He's been in town long enough tonight. Remember, I said to put him on his horse, not dump him in the slough!"

He went out then, as quietly and purposefully

as he had entered, a lean, erect, flat-backed man who left behind him an uneasy silence. Finally a man cleared his throat.

"Maybe Cole Logan might have fist-whipped him, but don't nobody make any mistake about it. There walks a man. For he sure just now cut Rack down to size, definite and complete. Yes, sir—he sure took all the growl out of Rack!"

VI—Uneasy Tides

There were areas of muscle that were board stiff when Dan Scoville crawled out of his blankets to face a new day, but, aside from these and the inevitable soreness that lay behind them, he felt much his usual self. By the time he had dressed, shaved carefully, and washed up, and had his breakfast at Mrs. Tyce's place, a lot of this stiffness had begun to wear off. There was a core of hard, wiry resilience in this man and a deep well of natural vigor to draw on. His pipe going, he sauntered out of the eating house and lazed along the street, welcoming the sun's first warmth.

Down by Ed Jethro's stable, Sage and Jethro were hooking a team to the stage, and Scoville's idle steps took him that way. Both men favored him with quick nods which carried a definite respect. And a moment later when the team was in place and ready to go, and Ed Jethro went back into the stable, Sage turned to Scoville and spoke with a low, hard emphasis.

"You should have killed him! You had every excuse. He was going for his gun, so I hear. Yeah, you should have killed him."

"What would that have proven, Sage? My job isn't killing people. But it is knocking some sense into thick heads."

Sage cut an emphatic hand across in front of him. "You've just cut by fifty per cent your chances of living to old age. You might gun-whip some men and leave 'em wiser and better men. But when you buffalo such as Rack Logan and don't finish the job, then you've set a mad animal loose on your trail."

Scoville peered off at nothing through pinched eyes. "You're a little hard to figure, Sage. On one hand, you lay out some pretty broad hints that while Cole Logan may have his faults, he's still a pretty good man. On the other hand, you seem to figure cousin Rack as being just no damn good."

"Which he ain't!" declared Sage vehemently. "Cole Logan is one man, Rack's another. Just because they're cousins is no reason why they should be exactly alike, is it? Well, they sure as hell ain't! They're different as night and day."

"How does it happen that they get along, then?"

"Two reasons. Cole's the boss, which Rack damn well knows. When Cole lays down the law to Rack, why Rack listens. Then, I reckon, there's some kind of family or clan loyalty mixed in. The Logan family's been long on this island. There's quite a slather of them, this way and that, and I guess Cole, he figures he's got to more or less take care of the whole lot. And Rack is one of the lot. All of which still don't make Rack anything but what he is, a mean, treacherous, no good—!"

"You think then," broke in Scoville, "that Cole

Logan might have sent Rack into town last night to give me a currying?"

"Didn't say that," retorted Sage, climbing to the box of the stage and sorting out the reins. "All I said was that you should have rubbed Rack out while you had the good chance. Because now, sure as you're a foot high, you'll have to do it one of these days, providing you're lucky enough to live that long. You got any word you want sent out to Riverton? I'm heading there."

Scoville shook his head. "Only word I got for you, Sage—is thanks! For last night and for the advice this morning."

He smiled faintly up at Sage as he said this. Sage rolled his morning cud of blackstrap in one leathery cheek, spat, and growled, "If I live to be a thousand, mebbe I'll learn to keep my fool mouth shut! You, Barney—Star—! Hup—hup!"

Sage kicked off the brake, and the stage made its complaining turn in the street and pulled up in front of Bill Profitt's store. Bill Profitt came out, tossed a mail bag up to Sage, traded a few remarks. Then the stage rolled on, made the turn up to the levee road, and racked out to the west, leaving behind the smell of morning's dust, newly churned up.

Dan Scoville went into the stable, sought out Ed Jethro, who was mending a set of harness. "You gave me a bargain on that gelding, Ed," said Scoville. "A mighty good horse."

Wispy little Ed Jethro considered a moment, then nodded. "Wanted you to have a good one. Could come a time when you'll need a good bronc under you—need it bad." He ran a lump of beeswax up and down a length of thread. "Bronc's in the big box stall out back. Tod Neely's there, giving the animal a currying."

Scoville moved on into the depths of the stable, considering the significance of Jethro's words. In his way, he thought, he was warning me, too.

Tod Neely was working industriously with currycomb and brush. Scoville leaned his crossed arms on the edge of the stall. "Owe you something, Tod—for taking care of my horse."

The boy's answer was low-toned. "You don't owe me nothin', Dan. I like to work around horses."

Scoville peered more keenly through the stable's gloom. Something in the boy's manner, in the tone of his voice, was somehow off key. Scoville kept silent, watching. Tod, finished on one flank of the gelding, moved around to work on the other. He limped a little as he moved.

Scoville's eyes narrowed. "What's the matter with your leg, Tod?"

The lad did not answer right away. Then, in gruff boyishness, "Nothing—nothing much. Just—bumped it."

It was Scoville's turn to be silent for a time. When he finally spoke his tone was casual.

"When you get through with the horse, Tod—come on over to the office."

It was half an hour later before the boy showed. He was definitely trying not to limp as he sidled in. But he could not hide the bruise on the side of his face. A glinting flash leaped into Dan Scoville's eyes, and his voice ran crisp as he brought aloud a conclusion he'd already arrived at.

"This Maze Dickson can turn mean, can't he, Tod—when he gets full of liquor?"

The boy started slightly, flashed Scoville a quick glance, then stared at the floor. "Sometimes," he admitted finally.

"Slapped you around, maybe—and kicked you?"

Tod bobbed his head up and down. "I can take it," he mumbled.

"Why did he rough you up, Tod?"

The boy shifted restlessly. "He—he kept saying something that wasn't so, and when I told him it wasn't—then he got mad."

Scoville had another flash of intuition. "Laying me out, wasn't he?"

Tod bobbed his head again. "Some. It wasn't right and I told him that. So—then—" He shrugged and said again, "I can take it."

"You don't have to take it," Scoville said quietly. "The other day I told you that you could hang out with me, any time you wanted to.

There's plenty of room in here to set up another bunk. I spoke to Bill Profitt about that, yesterday, and he said it was all right with him. How about it, Tod—wouldn't you like to move in with me?"

The boy's eyes came up, held Scoville's steadily. "Yeah, Dan—I would. I sure would—I'll work. And I won't get in your way. I—I—!" Tod's voice thickened and he gulped.

Scoville got quickly up from his chair. He spoke heartily to cover the boy's emotion. "That's fine—fine! We'll make a good pair, you and me. I reckon Bill Profitt can scare up that extra bunk. We'll go speak to him about it now, and while you help him get things squared away in here, I'll go collect your gear at the shanty boat."

Climbing the levee slope and dropping down past the wharf, Dan Scoville's steps quickened and the glint in his eyes kept getting colder and colder. There was no sign of life around the shanty boat, but as Scoville stepped on the cluttered, dirty, short deck of the thing, he heard heavy, drunken snores inside. He had to duck his head to get through the low doorway. The rank smell of stale whiskey, stale human sweat, and several other unidentifiable but equally nauseous stenches struck his nostrils.

The gloom was as thick as the foul odors, for the windows were small and cluttered with cobwebs and grime. But Scoville made out Maze Dickson lying flat on his back in a tangle of filthy blankets on a narrow bunk. Dickson's mouth was open and he was gurgling and snorting in his drunken sleep. He was a very unlovely sight.

On a bench by a grease-smeared stove stood half a bucket of water. Dan Scoville picked this up and let Dickson have the entire contents full in the face. Dickson came awake in a flurry of coughing, heavy curses.

"Damn you, Tod! Damn your ornery soul! Sluice me with water, will you. I'll break your damned back. I'll—"

Dickson had been pawing at his face with a dirty hand, mopping the water from his bleared eyes while he raged. Now he suddenly realized who it was that stood over him, empty pail in hand. His cursing tirade broke off abruptly, and he stared and blinked, then sought more words in a blustering mumble.

"What's the idea? Who—I thought it was that worthless kid, Tod Neely. I thought—"

"You thought wrong!" snapped Dan Scoville. "I got something for you, Dickson. Up on your feet!"

Instead of obeying, Maze Dickson's booze-bleared eyes went cunning and shifty. One hand began fumbling among the blankets and suddenly there was a knife in it, a long, heavy-bladed, wicked-looking thing.

"You touch me," blurted Dickson thickly, "you touch me, and—!"

That was as far as Dickson got before Scoville's bunched right knee smashed into his chest, knocking him back against the wall. Then Scoville dropped on him, grabbing the wrist of the knife hand and bending Dickson's arm across the side of the bunk until he bawled with pain and dropped the knife. Then, locking a hand in the front of Dickson's undershirt, Scoville stepped back and hauled the fellow to his wobbling feet.

"This, for Tod!" gritted Scoville.

He slapped Maze Dickson across the side of the face with his open right hand, slapped him so hard the sound was almost like a report. He slapped him again, backhanded and full-handed, slapped him until Dickson's shaking jowls turned crimson and his eyes stuck out and his head rolled soggily back and forth. Slapped him until Dickson's knees began to buckle and sag. Then he spun the dazed shanty-boater around and swung an emphatic boot. "That for Tod, too!"

The force of the kick drove Dickson floundering and reeling into the far wall of the shanty boat, where he struck with a crash, clawed wildly for support, missed it, spun around and came down in a heavy sprawl.

Scoville stood over him. "Stay right there," he ordered harshly. "Fold those filthy paws across that fat belly of yours and stay right there! I'm collecting Tod's gear, if there is any, and taking it out of this hogpen—just like I'm taking Tod out of here. For Tod's going to bunk with me from now on. And if you ever run into the lad anywhere again, at any time, and so much as say a word to him or lay a finger on him, then I'll really work you over!"

Tod had little enough in the way of belongings, and what there was had little value except for the sense of possession they'd given him, the feeling that he actually owned some small thing in a world that was very big and very uncertain for an orphaned youngster.

But what there was Scoville gathered up carefully. Then, as he moved past Dickson, he gave the fellow another contemptuous glance and went out without further words. When he reached the open air, he spat overside into the brown slough water, as though clearing his tonguc of a foul taste.

Molly Profitt was standing in his office door when he got back there. "Tod's gone down to Ed Jethro's to fill his bedtick with straw," she said. "That worthless Maze Dickson abused the boy, didn't he? I couldn't get Tod to tell me much about it. He's an intense little chap. And the person who finally wins that boy's full loyalty will have something to treasure all the rest of his days."

Scoville put Tod's gear on the table, then turned back to Molly Profitt. "Dickson hit the kid, and kicked him, too. Just a damned drunken no-good brute. But I gave him back his own medicine—a good dose of it. He knows now how it feels to be slapped and kicked around."

Molly Profitt's eyes grew soft. "You're a good man, Dan Scoville."

Scoville fumbled for his pipe, his eyes shadowed and seeing the memory of an old, past grief. "There was a little brother, once," he said gravely. "He'd have been just about Tod's age if the diphtheria hadn't hit. And a man can get—lonely—"

The Circle Cross ranch house was plainly but soundly built, and stood on a slight rise in the long level of the island, a point of vantage which extended a man's view and invited the touch of any breeze which might be stirring. Then there were a pair of sycamores which spread an area of welcome shade across the porch. As he jogged up the slight slope toward the place, Dan Scoville saw three people sitting in the shade. These three were Mal Baine, his daughter Nora, and Loren Logan.

There was an iron ring set into the trunk of one of the sycamores, and Scoville put the claybank gelding up to this, stepped from the saddle, dabbed rein ends through the ring, then turned to the three, touching his hat.

"Miss Baine," he said, "how are you?"

Nora Baine looked at him gravely. "How do

you do, Mr. Scoville." She indicated the others. "This is my father—and Loren Logan."

Scoville put out a quick hand to Mal Baine. "Glad to know you, sir." He turned and fixed Loren Logan with steady eyes. "An honor, Miss Logan."

She acknowledged his words with a stiff, but uncertain nod, then stood up and turned to Nora Baine. "I'll be going along now, Nora."

Nora's objection was swift. "You haven't been here any time at all. And I've a hundred things to talk to you about. We'll go inside and give these men free rein." Her glance touched Scoville. "It was Dad you wanted to see, wasn't it?"

Scoville showed her a small smile. "Among others, yes."

He watched the two girls go into the ranch house, Loren Logan slightly the taller of the two. Lord! She was a lovely thing. . . .

Mal Baine's voice ran dryly. "Have a seat, Scoville."

Scoville took a chair, his glance running here and there. "Where's the watchdog?"

Mal Baine looked puzzled for a moment. Then he cleared his throat gruffly. "Oh, you mean Rack? You should know the answer to that. From all I hear, you weren't exactly gentle with that buffaloing. Right now Rack's a sick whelp."

Scoville swung his head. "Whelp?"

"Whelp! A mean, worthless one."

Scoville got out his pipe. "I find that impression surprisingly general. Which makes it harder than ever to understand Cole Logan."

"Rack's one of the clan," said Baine. "That's enough for Cole. He'll stick by his blood through hell-fire."

Scoville nodded, a wreath of smoke curling up about his lean head. "Which brings me, among other things, pretty much to the point of this visit. It's one of the several matters I want to talk to you about. I understand that you're a friend of Cole Logan's, Mr. Baine—just about his best friend. How much influence have you got with him?"

"In the way I think you're driving at, none at all, I'm afraid," said the cattleman. "You may recall that I tried to talk Cole out of forcing that mixup you had with him. I didn't get very far, did I?"

Scoville ran a hand over his face, where the dark stain of bruises still lingered. He grinned wryly. "No, you didn't. Sure took a going over, didn't I?" Slowly the grin faded and his jaw hardened. "If this thing could stop right there, I'd shake hands with Logan and forget it. But it's got to stop there. I won't take a second mauling of that kind. Logan's got to understand that. Next time, I don't give up my gun. No matter what the odds, they don't take that away from me. Wonder if you could get that point across with Logan?

And make him realize whichever way the cat jumps in a smokeout, he stands to surely lose."

Mal Baine nodded soberly. "Know what you mean," he admitted somberly, "and it's surely something I don't want to see take place, for the sake of a lot of people. If matters should come to that sort of a showdown, and you were to get him, that would be very bad. And if it came out the other way and he should get you, then it would be worse. For then Frank Ide would come down from Riverton with all the help he might need for the job and either rub Cole out or take him to Riverton and hang him. That's the picture, isn't it?"

"That's exactly it!" affirmed Scoville bluntly. "You'd think Logan would have sense enough to realize that."

Mal Baine sighed deeply. "Cole seems to have a blind spot there. Outside of that one thing he's a damn well-balanced man and a mighty fine one. Oh, to get along with Cole, you got to admit he's the boss. I found that out a long time ago. At times it hasn't been too easy to take, but when I think it over, all in all I got to admit he's done a pretty good job of running things on Middle Island."

"Could be a mite of argument there," Scoville said briefly. "The day I came to Delta I saw a good example of Cole Logan's methods at work. I saw a scared and insignificant man and his weary and hopeless wife pushed around pretty roughly. Do you figure it necessary that Logan throw his weight at a fellow like Bid Hazen? If he was a rough, tough, dangerous sort, I might have understood it. But Hazen is anything but that. I can't imagine a less impressive specimen. At the same time, he's got his rights. One of them is that he doesn't have to live in eternal fear of any man, or that man's threats of hanging and such. And that includes Cole Logan."

Mal Baine spat beyond the edge of the porch, his expression hardening. "If you'd lived on this island as long as I have, Scoville—you'd see Bid Hazen and his kind through a different set of glasses. Damned shiftless breed. You find them in their cabins and shanty boats along the sloughs all around this island, and all through this delta country, for that matter. They're too damned lazy to do an honest lick of work. I'll bet a sizable chunk of money right now that if you were to be able to investigate their past records, nine out of ten of them have been mixed up in some sort of previous rascality somewhere, and they're using the delta country as a hideout."

"That," admitted Scoville, "may be true. But what proof have you that Bid Hazen isn't that tenth one? In any case, rascals or not, it's not Cole Logan's place to assume to a feudal lordship over their lives and affairs. I tried to make him see that the first time I had a brush with him, the day I arrived in Delta. I told him then that if he had any kind of legitimate criminal charge against Hazen that he wanted to press in a legitimate manner, I'd see that Hazen was taken out to Riverton to stand trial."

"Strictly proper on your part," growled Mal Baine, "but damned impractical. You forget, Scoville, that until you showed up with that star, the kind of law you represent had never really shown up or taken any interest in affairs here on Middle Island. To keep things in hand, we've had to do our own law-enforcing, and the chore has fallen to Cole Logan. Now, to get back to Bid Hazen and his kind. Like I told you, they're too lazy to work. Their idea is to live off the country, on the fish they catch out of the sloughs and the small game that they shoot. Sometimes they pick up a dollar or two by running a trap line along the levees. All of which wouldn't bother Cole Logan or me or anybody else if they'd stick to just that. But they don't. Hazen and his kind get a taste for fresh beef entirely too damned often!"

"Logan charged Hazen as a meat thief, a slow-elker," admitted Scoville.

Mal Baine leaned forward in his chair for emphasis. "And Cole's right! A lot of our beef critters have a way of disappearing all too regularly, and then, should you ride the levees, you have no trouble smelling beef meat frying or roasting. Even an occasional critter going that way, Cole and I might stand for. But when they begin disappearing a dozen or fifteen in a bunch, that's a little too rich for our blood. Hell! Cole and I even tried this idea. We offered to slaughter a beef regularly and put the meat up for sale through Bill Profitt's store at a rock-bottom price. It was just a waste of breath. You never saw a shanty-boater buy anything he figured he could steal!"

Scoville fixed the cattleman with a level glance. "Are you trying to tell me that Bid Hazen alone got away with a dozen head of cattle at one throw?"

"No, not alone. I'm just saying that's the way we've had our beef disappearing. But I do know, for a fact, that Cole Logan caught Bid Hazen with damn near a whole haunch of fresh beef on his hands. When Cole asked him where he got it, Hazen clammed up and wouldn't say a word. That's when Cole ran him off the island."

Scoville leaned over and tapped the dottle from his pipe against the leg of his chair. "And you yourself have lost cattle that way and in that amount?"

"I sure as hell have," growled Baine. "As high as three dozen in one year. Was it five or six, I'd still be able to hold my temper about it, but thirty-five or forty head takes a big bite out of a season's profit. And Cole Logan's been hit heavier than me, for he runs more cattle than anybody else on the island, and controls the biggest chunk of range."

"How about Ward Requa?" asked Scoville. "Does he lose any?"

Mal Baine frowned into the distance. "That I don't know anything about. Requa keeps his affairs to himself."

Scoville shot another keen glance at Baine. "Requa and Cole Logan don't get along too well, do they?"

Mal Baine seemed to retreat behind a mask of grimness. "I'm no hand at gossip," he said bluntly. "Anything that's between Cole and Requa is their business and none of mine. I don't see much of Requa. He seems to prefer minding his own business pretty strict, so I let him."

Scoville slowly tamped fresh tobacco into the bowl of his pipe. "In general, how do fellows like Bid Hazen go about getting away with your beef?"

The cattleman leaned back in his chair again. "Easy enough for them. Beef critters drift, hunt shade on hot days. That means they'll gang up on the levees where most of the tree growth is. There are plenty of lonely stretches along the levees; a rancher would need an army of men to patrol them all the time. So Hazen or one of his kind spots a couple of critters hunting shade on a levee. Nobody is around. So they slip up in a rowboat, shoot the critters, and butcher them right there. They dump the hides and offal into the slough, load the meat in their boat, and get out of there. Then, for the next two or three weeks, a lot of human swamp and tule rats live high. While the cattleman is out the price of a couple more fat critters he's worked and sweat to raise."

Dan Scoville was thoughtfully silent for a time, puffing his pipe. "Pretty tough to prove anything against anybody in a case of that sort," he said finally.

Mal Baine snorted. "Try and prove it! You locate some shanty-boater digging into a meal of good beef. You ask him where he got it. He'll tell you that a friend of his, another cabin- or shanty-boater gave it to him. So you tackle this next guy and ask him where he got the meat. He passes you on to another generous friend. And so it goes until you find yourself just chasing your tail in a circle. The only answer, as Cole Logan sees it—and I'm not saying he's wrong, either—is that when you find a tule rat eating good beef that he can't prove he got hold of legitimate, you run him off the island. That's what Cole aimed to do with Bid Hazen."

"Hasn't there ever been an occasion when one of these tule rats, as you call them, has been caught cold in the act of slow-elking?" Scoville asked.

"Two or three times, yes."

"What happened then?"

Mal Baine gave Scoville a direct, truculent stare. "Why they got the most direct and effective cow-thief medicine ever devised by man. A rope and a tree."

"Like Jack Neely, perhaps?" suggested Scoville softly.

"No! Not Jack Neely. Neither Cole Logan nor I had anything to do with that affair. Neely was just another shanty-boater, no better or worse than any of the others. He ate our beef, all right. In fact, Cole caught him with fresh beef in his possession, just like he did Bid Hazen. Cole gave him hell about it, but that was all. It was as big a surprise to Cole and me as to anybody else when we got word that Neely was found floating in Cross Over Slough with a rope still around his neck and a bullet hole in him. We certainly had nothing to do with that."

"You understand, of course," Scoville said, quietly, "that this lynch-rope stuff is out—completely! It might have been appropriate medicine in the old days, when no other immediate answer was to be had. But it definitely won't do any more. It was an affair of that sort which got George Delbert to sounding off."

Again Mal Baine spat across the porch edge. "That damned big-mouthed shyster!"

"And," murmured Scoville, "somebody took a shot at him."

"So he claimed," growled Mal Baine. "If it's true, then I'm not too sure it wasn't a pity they missed him."

There was a patter of hoofs at the far corner of the ranch house, and then Loren Logan, up on that fine black horse of hers, rode into view, cutting out into the main ranch trail and heading out along it without a backward look.

Dan Scoville stood up. "You've supplied quite a few parts of a picture for me, Mr. Baine. For that, thanks. And if you can do anything toward bringing Cole Logan to common sense on this question of authority, then double thanks. When you hit town, drop in at the office and make yourself at home."

Scoville went over to his horse, swung up, and headed down the trail after Loren Logan.

Nora Baine came out of the house and stood beside her father's chair. Mal Baine was staring after Dan Scoville with scowling intentness. "If that fellow Scoville tries to make up to Loren, that will set Cole off—plenty!" he growled.

Nora Baine's eyes showed a cast of apprehension. "I don't see why it should, Dad. I hope not. For one thing, Dan Scoville is a complete gentleman. And I'm sure that what he wants to do more than anything else is reach a basis of friendship with everybody on Middle Island who counts. As far as Loren is concerned, she's never asserted herself to Cole. But that doesn't mean that she won't. Today is the first time she's ever ridden away from home without Rack trailing after her. I'm sure she's enjoyed the sense of freedom it's given her. Something else, Dad. I think that Loren, more than anyone else, once she sets her mind to it, can control Cole and bring him to an understanding of a new state of affairs."

"I hope so," grunted Mal Baine. "For there'll be no backing up in that fellow Scoville."

Within less than half a mile of the Circle Cross headquarters, Dan Scoville had drawn up to a yard or two of the black horse and its rider. He knew that the girl ahead of him was well aware of his approach, and knew also that if she had wanted to she could easily have run away from him. For, good a horse as the claybank gelding was, it wasn't in the class of the black. But the girl was too proud, apparently, to lift her mount to a faster pace; so, a little farther on, Scoville drew even with her. Faint flags of color lay in the girl's cheeks, but her head was high and her gray eyes fixed straight ahead. Scoville spoke quietly.

"I'm meaning no offense of any kind in this, you understand, Miss Logan. I rode out to join you because there are a few things I want to talk over with you."

She did not answer, nor did she look at him. Scoville studied her. Her beauty was as breathtaking as ever and her every move was soft grace as she answered to the swing of her mount. Abruptly Scoville's settled scrutiny got reaction which his words had not. She turned slightly in her saddle.

"You've no right to do this—ride with me, speak to me. I did not ask you to."

"No," conceded Scoville gravely, "you didn't ask me to ride with you. But I told you why I chose to do so, anyway. And in the pursuit of my duties I've the right to approach and speak to anyone and to question them respectfully, as I do with you now. And I might add that it's to the benefit of the Logan family that you listen to me and answer those questions."

She flared a little. "Are you trying to threaten me? Well, I don't care to listen to you or answer any questions. I don't know you and I don't want to."

Had Dan Scoville been viewing this from a more impersonal point of view, he might have guessed a certain confused uncertainty behind Loren Logan's words and attitude. But it was impossible for Scoville to be near this girl and speak to her with any impersonal feeling. The impact of her beauty and personality upon him was too great. From anyone else, her words and manner would have meant nothing to him. But from this girl they for some reason carried a bite which reached deep and stirred a queer anger in him. Harshness came into his tone.

"I'm trying to believe that somewhere in the Logan family I'll strike a vein of common sense, but I'm beginning to believe it's a false hope. What kind of a crazy, twisted world have you all been living in, anyhow? Who sold you the idea that you're a queen that no man can speak to, or look at? I marvel that they let you get away today without some kind of watchdog hanging at your heels!"

Hot color flamed and faded, flamed and faded in her face. She gathered her reins slightly. "I think," she struck back, "that I'm glad Cole gave you that beating!"

In the next moment she would have lifted the black to a run, but Scoville shot out an arm, grabbed the bit ring of the black, and hauled the animal to a whirling halt, halfway through its first lunge.

"I'll talk and you'll listen!" gritted Scoville. "No, don't try and use that quirt on me, or I'll have to lay rough hands on your sacred person!"

She paid no attention to his warning. Twice she lashed at him with her quirt, and twice Scoville caught the stinging lash across the spread, upthrust palm of his free hand, trying to grip the use-slickened, hard-braided leather. The second time he succeeded. The rawhide loop of the quirt was around her right wrist, and when Scoville, his own grip secure, jerked at the quirt, he hauled her half out of her saddle. In this short moment of confused struggle, the claybank and the black had swung side by side, close together, and so, of a sudden, Dan Scoville found this girl almost leaning against him, almost in his arms.

Her gray eyes, half frightened, half wildly angry, were only inches from his own, blazing with fury. As Scoville slackened his pull on the quirt, she made use of the slack to slip her hand free of the loop and regained her balance in the saddle.

"Cole," she choked, "Cole will kill you for this!"

"And hang if he does," shot back Scoville. "Hang by the neck until he's dead, so help him God! Consider that picture and see if you like it!"

She did not seem to hear him. She was staring past him, out to the east. And now, in place of the anger in her voice, it was fear that reached out.

"Cole—there he comes, now! He saw this—he won't understand—! He'll be crazy mad. And shooting—there mustn't be shooting—! What can I do—what can I do?"

Scoville swung the claybank away, looked as she was looking. And he saw what she saw—Cole Logan, coming in on them at a wild run.

A gray and dismal foreboding settled over Dan Scoville. He settled himself in his saddle, his right hand dropping and brushing past the holstered gun at his hip.

VII—The Stranglers

Cole Logan closed in fast, his horse spurred to a lather. He sat solid and square and dominant in his saddle, and under the wind-flattened brim of his hat his face was dark and cold. Ten yards away he set his mount up in a rearing, dust-scattering halt, and his voice lashed out, hoarse with the fury in him.

"Loren—get out of here! Get on home. I'll have an understanding with you, later. You wouldn't listen to me—you would sneak away by yourself. Now you got the answer—being mauled by this damned star-packer. Where's your pride—your common sense? You hear me—get out of here!"

The sheer impact of Cole's fury and his personality made the girl start to obey. But then she spun the black back and held her ground. "No! I won't leave. You don't understand, Cole. It was my fault. He—he meant nothing wrong. Cole—you must listen to me. You must—!"

Cole did not seem to hear her, seemed now to have put her completely out of his mind. His savage glance, his every faculty, centered on Dan Scoville.

"You!" he raged. "I gave you your chance. I should have killed you with my bare hands. I could have, but I gave you your warning. I told you to get off this island, but you didn't go. Instead, you cornered Rack and gun-whipped him. Now I catch you cold, trying to maul this fool sister of mine. Well, I make no more mistakes like that. This time it's final!"

Cole Logan went for his gun.

Dan Scoville had been watching this man with an alertness as fine and bright as a silver wire. And now, because of a previous judgment he had made, he took the longest and most dangerous gamble of his life. The judgment was based on what he had seen in many men before. Which was that men, bull powerful physically, instinctively depended more on that physical attainment in conflict than they did on other means. The weight of their fists, the power of their thews, were their primary weapons. And so, they were nearly always less dexterous and deadly with a gun than men of less physical power. It was the man who needed a gun to make himself a match for bigger men who made himself efficient and deadly with one. It was on this judgment that Scoville made his gamble.

So now he matched Cole Logan's draw and saw that he had guessed right. He was 'way ahead of Logan and, had he wished, could have laid a slug squarely in Cole's burly chest. Instead, he held his fire while he hauled on the claybank's near rein, digging in his spurs at the same moment.

And the claybank lunged aside, away from the girl, angling toward Cole's right.

Cole's gun came up and roared its report, but the wildly wheeling lunge of Scoville's mount carried him clear. Once more Scoville could easily have driven a slug into Logan. Instead, he sent a harsh yell rocketing.

"You stupid fool! Put down that gun! Don't make me kill you!"

As he yelled, Scoville drove his mount boring in on Logan, who, paying no attention to Scoville's warning cry, twisted in his saddle, throwing his gun high before chopping down for a second try. Before he could get it away, Scoville's charging mount smashed a shoulder into Cole's horse, knocking it sideways and back. And Scoville, standing high in his stirrups and leaning far forward, swung his own gun in a slashing arc. His aim was at Cole's forearm, not his head, and the aim was good. The heavy gun barrel thudded home with numbing effect, driving Cole's gun from his nerveless fingers, to drop harmlessly to the ground.

Again Scoville sent the claybank smashing into Cole's horse, nearly knocking that animal from its feet. Then, as Cole's horse floundered to get its balance, Scoville quieted the claybank and dropped his gun back into the holster, and stared at Cole in gray and bitter fury.

"You fool! You complete, pigheaded fool! I

don't know why I held back—I tell you I don't know! But I never will again, Logan—never! I've made my last allowance to you. You better believe that. Do you understand? I'll never hold back again. You ever come at me again with a gun and you'll get what you ask for!"

Two things cut through Cole Logan's black rage. One was Dan Scoville's blast of words. The other was that this lean, cold-eyed deputy had been 'way ahead of him with a gun, that he was alive now only because that deputy had deliberately withheld his fire; that he had had first chance and missed, and that the man he had shot at had refused to shoot back. And it was this last that really crushed him. For it cut the very heart out of the black and ravening Logan pride.

Cole Logan swung his head from side to side, licked his lips, finally brought his glance to meet Dan Scoville's icy stare. Scoville spoke again, his voice a honed knife of harshness.

"The Logans—the great, all-powerful Logans! I heard about them back in Riverton. I heard about them at the Spanish Slough ferry, and I heard about them along the stage road and in Delta. I heard of a man named Cole Logan who would be God, and who would assume the authority of handing out life and death to other men. I heard of the beautiful Loren Logan, who rode like a queen and who was always guarded by a surly whelp named Rack Logan. Yeah, Mister Rack

Logan, who stood ready to smash down any ordinary mortal who so much as dared to look at, or speak to the great lady. Oh, I heard plenty about the Logans!"

He paused, driving a clenched fist against his saddle horn before going on.

"So now the Logans are going to hear from me. I'll take care of their strut and swagger. I'll cut the high pride out of them. From now on, when I meet up with a Logan, he gets off the trail, not me. From now on I'll blind them with this star I carry. I'll make them tip their damned hats when they pass it. Tough, they fancy themselves. By God—from now on they're going to find out just what real toughness is!"

With this final word, Dan Scoville lifted the claybank gelding to a run and surged away.

For a long moment there remained no sound except the snorting and blowing of Cole's hard-run horse. Then came a choked sob from Loren Logan, and a mumbled curse from Cole. He followed this with growling, but almost aimless words.

"No need of that—no need of that. Where's your pride?"

Loren's head came up and she lashed back at him. "You should speak of pride—you should, Cole Logan! He could have killed you, but he didn't. He could have shot you dead—but he didn't. He was generous where—where you were a fool! Pride! What do you mean by the word?"

Again Cole swung his heavy head from side to side, like a trapped and bewildered bear. "He laid hands on you," he mumbled. "He was trying to maul you. I saw that. And I'll go after him and—"

The girl brushed a hand across her eyes. "Stop it!" she cried. "Stop that kind of bluster and empty talk! You don't know how stupid it sounds after—after just now. Can't you understand what has happened? He could have killed you, I say. And with every right, for you had drawn a gun on him. Yes, he could have killed you—but he didn't. Doesn't that mean anything to you?"

Dull color burned in Cole's face. "I'm not afraid of him. Maybe he could have killed me—but I'm still not afraid of him."

"Being afraid or not afraid has nothing to do with it," Loren stormed. "But being sensible for a change has everything to do with it. As usual, you jumped at conclusions. Dan Scoville wasn't trying to lay hands on me, or maul me, as you put it. All he did was take my quirt away from me because I struck at him with it. And I had no right to do that. I was wrong and he was right." She paused and drew a deep breath before going on.

"And he was right in what he just said to both of us. He spoke the truth about we Logans. We've been living in an arrogant fool's paradise. Or rather, a fool's hell. And I, for one, will have no more of it. The authority on this island isn't you, or any other Logan. It's Dan Scoville and what he represents. That's something you're going to have to understand, Cole—now and for all the future!"

Cole Logan had never seen his sister like this before. Always before she had been content to let him handle all problems, to bow to his authority and his judgment. But this was open rebellion. He tried to regain a control he felt slipping away from him.

"You're upset right now, Loren," he said gruffly. "And naturally enough. But there was an obligation handed down to me that still holds good and—"

"Obligation be—be darned!" she cut in furiously. "Call it what it really is—a silly, overbearing idea of false greatness. Has it ever occurred to you how foolish that idea must have made the Logans appear in the eyes of saner folks? Well, it never did to me, either—until now. Now I'm ashamed, and I feel very small and ridiculous. When were the Logans ever so generous to anyone as Dan Scoville was to you, just a few minutes ago? All he did was hand you back your life after you'd done your best to take his away from him. If that one thing doesn't open your mind, then nothing ever will."

Again she brushed a hand across her eyes. "Here is something else, Cole. From now on I ride where I please and when I please. And alone, if that's the way I want it. There'll be no more of Rack, or anyone else, trailing after me like some snarly watchdog. I'm tired of being paraded as some sort of superior, precious untouchable. I'm no better or worse than any other woman. And that's the way I want to be."

She straightened in her saddle, squared her slender shoulders. "Now I'm going home! And so are you."

She spurred off. For a time Cole Logan sat staring after her. Unconsciously his left hand settled on his right forearm and he rubbed it up and down, massaging at the spot when Dan Scoville's gun barrel had landed. Cole looked down, his glance searching the earth for his gun. He swung heavily from the saddle and recovered the weapon. Then he went back astride and, with his head sunk in moody introspection, set off after his sister, riding at a jog.

The worst of the fires of anger had burned out of Dan Scoville by the time he got back to Delta. But the passing of that gray burst of fury had left him as it always did, feeling letdown and scorched inside. It was the inevitable reaction. A shadow of morose taciturnity settled on him and held while he stabled the claybank and then went over to the office.

Coming up to the door of the place, Scoville

heard a small boy's whistling, somewhat off key, and then Tod Neely showed, wielding a broom. At the look on Scoville's face, the boy turned silent, sober. Scoville forced a grin.

"Still chasing dust, Tod? Thought we'd got rid of the worst of it."

"We did," agreed the lad. "But some keeps sneakin' in. And after the way it was on Maze Dickson's shanty boat, I figure I just can't keep things too clean in here." He gave Scoville another long, sober appraisal. "Something wrong, Dan?"

"The world," said Scoville gruffly, "is full of fools, Tod. You're looking right at one."

The boy considered this for a moment, then shook his head gravely. "I don't think so, Dan. Others, maybe—but not you."

The harsh wall in Scoville began to crumble and his face softened. A small boy's loyalty and worship. If a man had that, then he possessed something no amount of money could buy. And it would be something to live up to. He dropped a hand on Tod's shoulder.

"Thanks for coming to live with me, Tod."

He lowered himself into a chair and reached for his pipe. "All right, Tod—say I was just part fool. Now about something else. The other day you said something about being able to get hold of a boat. What kind of a boat and whose is it?"

"It's a skiff—fourteen-footer. It's mine. Leastways, I found it. Found it drifted into some tules. Been there a long time, looked like. Had a busted plank and was full of water. I drug it out and fixed it up and painted it. I run errands for Bill Profitt to earn a pair of oars. I got it stashed away in the tules down the slough a bit. I never let on to Maze Dickson that I had it, or he'd likely have taken it away from me and sold it to buy likker. Why do you ask, Dan? You want to go fishin'?" Eagerness was in Tod's eyes as he finished.

"Maybe, one of these days," Scoville answered, frowning with thought. "Or maybe, just for a long ride some time. I'd say the boat was certainly yours, Tod. So you don't have to keep it stashed away in the tules. You can bring it up and tie it right alongside of the wharf, same as any other boat owner."

The gleam in the boy's blue eyes deepened. "I'd sure like to do that, Dan. I don't like to have to sneak around with anything."

"Then," said Scoville, "soon's you finish sweeping out, you go get your boat. And don't you ever sneak, Tod. You stand right on your own two feet and look the world in the eye."

It didn't take the boy long to finish with the sweeping. Then he left at a run, his bare feet twinkling. Quiet settled in the office, but only for a moment. For there was the sound of hoofs and the creak of leather thoroughbraces along the street outside, and Sage brought his dusty

Concord to a halt in front of Bill Profitt's store door.

Dan Scoville moved out on the porch, caught Sage's eye, lifted a hand in greeting. "Dry run, Sage?" he called.

Sage climbed down, came along the porch, searching in a pocket. He held out an envelope. "For you. Frank Ide sent it. Got a passenger, too. George Delbert. Seems all I do is haul back folks that Cole Logan's run off the island at one time or another. Cole's liable to get real cross with me about that, one of these days."

Sage shot the inevitable stream of tobacco juice out into the street's dust, then clumped back and turned into the store. Scoville turned back into his office, ripping open the envelope. The enclosure was terse:

> DAN:
>
> *I hear George Delbert is heading back to Delta. For no good reason that I can figure out. So keep an eye on him. I still say he's just a fourth-grade shyster. If he gets in your way, give him a floater. Luck.*
>
> FRANK IDE

Scoville read the note a second time, then tore it to small bits and dropped these into the empty nail keg which Tod Neely had brought in to act as a catch-all. A moment later it was George

Delbert himself who stood in the office door.

He was of medium height, running somewhat to paunch. His eyes were as hard and shiny as brown bottle glass and slightly protuberant, which gave him a somewhat truculent look. He had a small hooked nose above a pettish, sarcastic mouth, and his face was florid.

"Profitt should have held this office for me," he said abruptly. "I told him I'd be back."

Dan Scoville shrugged. "Maybe Bill didn't understand you. Anyhow, I've staked the claim. Sorry."

Delbert was pompously stubborn. "Where else am I going to find office room in this town? There's space enough for two of us in here."

"Already two," drawled Scoville. "Tod Neely and me. Again—sorry." He swung his head, glanced at the inner wall. "That bullet hole is still there."

Delbert flushed, his mean mouth pulling. "Among other things, I understand you're here to cut Cole Logan down to size. High time. See that you do a job of it."

The lawyer turned and stamped off down the porch. Dan Scoville went into the rear room, stretched out on his bunk, and lost himself in a spell of thinking. A little later he dozed off.

Evening brought a whipping wind in from the west, and though it sent curling spirals of dust along the street, it had a coolness in it and the good smell of fog and the distant ocean. Dan Scoville faced it and relished its flavor, along with that of an after-supper cigar.

He and Tod Neely had had their supper at Mrs. Tyce's place, after which Tod had headed for Bill Profitt's store.

"Missis Profitt says it's high time I got some book learnin'," the boy explained before he left. "She's goin' to start me in at it tonight. All right with you, Dan?"

To which, of course, Scoville had given hearty approval. Watching the lad scurry off through the dusk, Scoville knew a warm current of inner satisfaction. If he'd done nothing else since arriving in this town, he'd given this boy a boost along a healthy trail of life.

Later, the wind developed enough of a chill to drive Scoville to the shelter of his office, and there Ward Requa found him.

"Hear George Delbert is back in town," said Requa, settling in a chair and rolling a smoke. Then he added, with his small, cynical grin, "He must have forgotten about that bullet hole in yonder wall."

"He was in here," admitted Scoville. "I reminded him of it, but I don't think he appreciated the fact."

Requa's smile became a soundless chuckle. "Must be that star of yours that gave him the courage to come back. He'll expect you to mother him. Great one for standing on his constitutional rights, George is. Wave the flag, sing 'The Star-Spangled Banner.' Down with this, up with that. All that sort of thing, you know."

Scoville rolled his cigar reflectively across his lips. "There's one angle I can't help wondering about, Requa. What is there for a lawyer in this town? I may be wrong, but from where I sit I'm damned if I can see enough business for a lawyer to keep him from starving to death."

Ward Requa shrugged. "Don't ask me. A long time since, I've given up trying to understand people and why they do this or why they do that." He cocked an appraising eye. "For that matter, I can't figure you."

Scoville met Requa's glance through a coiling film of cigar smoke. "How's that?"

"Why," said Requa slowly, "they tell me that the other night in the Wagon Wheel, you had Rack Logan dead to rights. Dead to rights and with every justification in the world to kill him. Yet you only walloped him across the head with your gun and let it go at that. No, I can't figure you."

Scoville's answer ran a little crisp. "My friend, I wasn't sent in here to gun every would-be tough hombre I meet up with. For that matter, my personal tastes don't run to gunwork, either. No, I'm not here to start a gun feud. Rather, it's to head off that very thing and to get the people on this island educated to the fact that the way to settle their differences is through the channels of constituted law. That being the case, I'd sure set a fine example if I went around shooting holes in all those who disagree with me."

Requa got to his feet. "Now that's a noble theory, I suppose. But I can't think of a better way to make your life a short one with a quick end. You think Rack's going to forgive and forget? Or Cole, or any of the rest of the Logan gang, either?" Requa flipped his cigarette butt out of the open door, beyond which, in the outward pour of the lamplight, the first sliding coils of the oncoming fog were beginning to show.

"Strange as it may seem," drawled Scoville, "it may work out just that way. At least I'm hoping it will."

"You won't see it work that way here," retorted Requa bluntly. "You don't know the Logans—you haven't been around them long enough. Takes time to get the full picture of that outfit. Well, it's your business and your right to run it any way you want. Now, I think I'll locate George Delbert, buy him a couple of drinks, and then sit back and enjoy myself."

He caught the question in Scoville's eye, and grinned.

"George is a frustrated politician. Get a few shots of rye into him and he really starts to unwind. Gets off on his favorite subject—the rights of men. He turns real majestic. He'll pace the floor. He'll give you the Constitution of the United States, word for word, with Lincoln's Gettysburg Address thrown in for good measure. He'll quote Washington and Jefferson and Dan'l Webster. Oh, I tell you, it's a show. And all it costs you is the price of a couple of drinks."

Requa started to leave, paused in the doorway, and in an altered tone, said, "Don't forget Rack. You'd be a fool if you did."

Left alone, Scoville finished his cigar in sober thought; then, when a gust of fog swirled in at the open door, moved over to close the portal. For a few moments he stood, looking out at ocean's pale ghosts, blowing moistly through the street's darkness. Then, as he was about to close the door, a voice reached at him.

"Please! I'd like to speak to you, Mr. Scoville."

Scoville stood rooted in surprise. The voice was one that had stayed in his mind from the first moment he'd heard it. It belonged to Loren Logan.

She was a slim shadow, slipping in from the darkness and the fog, and as she moved past Scoville into the office, she brought the breath of the fog with her, along with a faint perfume.

Scoville closed the door, still mute with his surprise. She was in her divided riding skirt. There was a silk muffler about her throat and there was a buckskin jacket buttoned snugly up to her chin. She was bareheaded, and her dark hair was beaded with fog moisture which glinted in the lamplight like a silver mist. That same dampness lay on her cheeks and lips.

Immediately he sensed a strange excitement in her; it shone in her eyes and was reflected by the slightly breathless parting of her lips. It made him think of an eager child, half carried away by the thrill of an adventure. She met his wondering glance and color fanned her cheeks.

"If I seem just a trifle giddy, Mr. Scoville, it is because, for the first time in my life, I've ridden alone at night. And in the fog, too. And it's been a wonderful thrill."

"I can't," said Scoville slowly, "understand how your brother Cole allowed it."

"He wasn't home when I slipped away; he'd ridden off somewhere on some sort of ranch business." She tossed her head slightly. "Besides, from now on I ride where I please and when I please. I—" She stopped abruptly, and some of that little-girl eagerness faded. "I don't know why I should be saying these things to you. It wasn't what I came for."

"Then you did ride all the way to town to see me," murmured Scoville. "That's an honor I hardly expected—after this afternoon. After the things you said—and that I said."

Now she was completely grave, and some of

the cloak of the old, distant, imperious pride was back. She looked at him levelly.

"I came to see you because I felt that I was in your debt. And I wished to discharge that debt as best I could. Words are all I have to offer, and poor recompense for the generosity you showed me and Cole today. I want to say—that I thank you, greatly."

Scoville pushed a chair forward. "I'm forgetting my manners. You'll have to excuse me there, for I find myself completely dumbfounded. Five minutes ago, if I'd been asked to guess who would be the next person to come through this office door, you'd have been the last I'd have named. Won't you sit down?"

He moved on around the table, took his own chair, and then fumbled for his pipe while he tried to get his thoughts in order, and the fact that it was Loren Logan, in person, right here in front of him, into proper perspective.

The girl, who had sat down, was watching him now in complete silence. Scoville met her glance.

"This is a very gracious thing you do, Miss Logan. I'm not sure that I deserve it. I said some pretty bitter things out there today."

"And with every cause," was her quiet reply. "Though I'm hoping you did not mean everything you said, no more than I did. Like—like I was glad that Cole had given you that beating. I—I did not really mean that."

Scoville, more at ease now, smiled faintly. "Didn't think you did. You were mad then, and folks say lots of things when they're mad that they don't really mean."

A faint flag of color stole through her cheeks. "Then you didn't mean all you said? For you were very angry."

Scoville was silent while he got his pipe to going. He knew what she was referring to—his threat of really going for his gun if Cole or any other Logan ever crossed him again. His face hardened a little.

"There's a limit to a man's patience, Miss Logan. It's pretty tough to ask a man to put his life on the line and not defend it. From the first, I've tried to work on this thing through calm reason. There are some who don't seem to recognize the meaning of the word."

"You're referring to Cole, of course," she nodded. "I know I've no right to ask further forbearance on your part—yet I am asking it. If I can gain just a little more time—"

"What for? To really work on Cole, and make him see sense?"

"Yes. I gave him fits today. I told him how wrong he was, how wrong he'd been—how wrong the whole past Logan attitude had been. I think—no, I know I made an impression. And more than anything else, what stunned him was the realization that after he'd tried to—to shoot you, you refused to shoot back, when you could have so easily and with such certain effect. That shook him as nothing ever has before."

"If it did," said Scoville, "then the gamble I took was worthwhile." He added, somewhat somberly, "I'd hate to be asked to do it again, for I don't believe I'd be up to it. In a matter of that sort a man is largely guided by instinct alone, but sometimes that same instinct could throw the weight the opposite way."

Her voice ran low, hesitant, her eyes cast down at her nervously folded hands. "I wouldn't ask you to be that generous again, not even for Cole's sake. All I'm asking is a little further patience with a very stubborn, strong-minded, but fundamentally very good man—my brother. If you will do that, then it will give me time to work on him further and bring him to sensible understanding. I—I know I can do it, if I have the time."

Her head came up again and her gray eyes were moist with the same plea she'd just voiced. Dan Scoville got to his feet, took a couple of turns up and down the office. With a glance, this girl had the ability to shake him up inside like nothing he'd ever known before. It took effort on his part to keep his voice gruff.

"Let's cast this thing up, Miss Logan. The other day your brother Cole gave me a real man-to-man licking, as you well know. What did it prove?

Nothing, except that, physically, Cole is too tough a handful for me. I don't hold that against Cole. I've been licked before. It was Cole's way of trying to inflict his will on me and make me get off the island. It's a method that seems to have worked with others. But what Cole has got to get through his head is that it won't work with me."

He stopped in front of her, tall and lean and dark against the lamplight.

"What you've got to make Cole understand is that he can't win! Not by those tactics. Nor by any other except by coming around to sane reason. Cole must understand that if I didn't have the backbone to stand up to him, why then Sheriff Frank Ide would send somebody in who would. Today, had Cole made good on his gun try at me, then he'd have been just as surely dead as I was. For Frank Ide would have come down from Riverton, with an army of men if necessary, and he'd have taken Cole back to Riverton where the law would have hung him. That's the picture. That's all of it. It's not a pretty one, but it's still the picture. Certainly you don't want such a thing to happen, and certainly I don't, either. But it is what we must make Cole understand. That he can't win. If you'll work to make him see that, I'll certainly do everything I can to help you."

She stood up, moved toward the door. "You are more than generous, Dan Scoville. I'll bring Cole to his senses if—if I have to beat him. Thank you again."

She opened the door, and the fog was a gray-white boiling mist in the gush of lamplight. At her shoulder Scoville said, "Now Cole and I have a common worry—you riding home alone on a night like this. I'll get my horse and—"

"No!" she shook her head. "I've just found a freedom I want to enjoy and protect." Then she turned and gave him a swift and warming smile. "Some other time, Dan Scoville—!"

Then she was gone, into the fog, and it swallowed her instantly.

Scoville stood there, the door open, listening until hoofs made a faint and departing echo through the muffled night. He closed the door and went back to his chair. The office seemed queerly empty. Yet there lingered a faint breath of perfume. . . .

Well out along the home trail, it was Loren Logan's black horse that gave her the first inkling that other riders were abroad and close at hand. The black began tossing its head and snorting softly.

Swiftly the girl swung the animal off the trail, several yards back into the shelter of the fog-drenched blackness. She petted the black's arched neck, whispered to it, and the black quieted.

She heard the riders drift past on the trail, hoofs thumping, saddle gear creaking. And she heard a man drop a remark in a voice peculiarly hoarse and gravelly.

"This damned fog is good for something after all. It'll be a help on a job like this one—"

Loren waited until all sound of the riders was well past, then put the black back on the trail and resumed her solitary way.

Back in his office, Dan Scoville was finishing a final pipe when Tod Neely came trotting in, bringing with him a refreshing exuberance.

"Missis Profitt said I did real well for a start, Dan. She's having Bill send out for a flock of learnin' books for me." Then he added shyly, "Don't know if you get what I mean, Dan—but it sure makes a feller feel warm and comfortable to be alongside of Missis Profitt."

Scoville smiled gravely at thc lad. "I know exactly what you mean, Tod. You listen to what Mrs. Profitt has to teach you and you'll never go wrong."

They turned in for the night, shortly after that. Tod was soon asleep, and Scoville found a quiet comfort in listening to the youngster's soft breathing. Then, over and over again, the events of this day ran through his mind. He knew again a touch of the dark fire that had burned in him when he faced down Cole Logan, but this was quickly gone as he recalled a closer memory, that of Loren Logan when she had first stood in his office door, her lips and cheeks and hair fog-jeweled and all the fine sweet breath of the wide night clinging to her. . . .

It was still, black dark when he awoke. There was an unsteady, but insistent knocking at the outer office door. Scoville slid from under his blankets, pulled on his jeans and boots, slipped his gun from the holster where it hung at the head of his bunk, then felt his way to the outer door. He opened it to feel, but not see, the wet fog blowing.

The world was completely sunk in the blackness of the hours past midnight. The town was without a vestige of a light, sleeping. Scoville's voice ran low and curt.

"Who is it? What do you want?"

It was a tired voice that answered him, tired and numbed and full of dry tears and hopelessness.

"It—it's Missis Bid Hazen. They've hung my man—they've hung him—!"

VIII—Grisly Challenge

Dan Scoville helped Mrs. Bid Hazen inside. She was weak and uncertain, shaking from the night's wet chill and the emotional beating she had taken. He located the lamp and got it going and moved up a chair for the woman. She sank into this, her face drawn and gray, twisted with a dry grief which denied her the surcease of tears, and in her faded eyes was a fixed and almost unbelieving terror.

"Rest a little, ma'am," said Scoville gently. "I'll get some more clothes on and then I'll want all you can tell me. Try and get it all figured out straight."

The stir of it all had awakened Tod Neely, and Scoville was pulling on his shirt when Tod's sleepy voice came across the room to him.

"What is it, Dan—what's wrong?"

"Trouble, Tod," Scoville answered. "Things for you to do. Scramble out and dress and then go see if you can rouse Mrs. Profitt. Bring her into the office."

Tod was up and dressed in a scurry of motion and followed Scoville into the front office. He stared, silent and round-eyed, at the crumpled, gray-faced woman in the chair, and then, at a hastening nod from Scoville, slipped out into the dark.

For a little time Scoville was silent, hardly knowing how to go about questioning Mrs. Hazen. He had the feeling that anything he said would be laying the whip still farther across the bowed shoulders of this stricken, crushed woman. But he had to know. He cleared his throat a little gruffly.

"You said 'they' did it, Mrs. Hazen. Who do you mean by 'they'?"

For a long moment she did not answer. Then her words came, thin and lifeless. "I—I don't know. I don't know who they were. But they did it. They hung my man—my Bid. They hung him—I saw him there—swinging—"

She shuddered and her voice dried up. Her head sagged lower, and her bony, toil-harshened hands gripped and locked together, as though trying to find support. Abruptly she threw a folded arm across the table top, her head dropped on it, and the damned-up tears and grief broke in a storm of racking sobs.

Scoville stood in grim silence, knowing that this was the best thing that could happen—this release. The minutes ticked by, and the woman's grief was lessening slightly when there came a stir at the door and Tod Neely slipped in, followed by Molly Profitt in wrapper and slippers, her snowy hair tousled about her head. Scoville stepped over to her, explained in curt, softened tones.

He saw first bright anger, followed by soft compassion leap into Molly Profitt's eyes, and then she became all practical efficiency. She dropped a hand on Tod's shoulder.

"You go tell Bill I want him, Tod. Tell him to heat up the coffeepot and bring it and a cup along. Scoot!"

Tod scooted. To Scoville, Molly Profitt said, "Get me a couple of blankets, Dan."

Scoville stripped some off his bunk and these Molly Profitt wrapped around Mrs. Hazen's bowed figure, then pulled up a chair beside her, sat down, and put an arm around the stricken woman's shoulders. She began speaking softly, soothingly. Gradually she pulled the woman's head over on to her own warm, compassionate shoulder. Dan Scoville waited.

By the time Tod and Bill Profitt showed, Mrs. Hazen had quieted. At Molly Profitt's command, Mrs. Hazen gulped a cup of steaming black coffee. It warmed and steadied her. Her head came up and she looked at Dan Scoville.

"You have the authority," she quavered. "You'll go after them? You'll see that they're punished—for this?"

Scoville tipped his head. "Of course. But first, I've got to know who to go after. You can help me there, Mrs. Hazen, by telling me all you know."

"That's right," seconded Molly Profitt softly. "You must tell him."

So Mrs. Hazen, a little haltingly at first, then in steadying words, told her story. The Hazen shanty boat was tied up at Heron Point, some six miles east of town along Cross Over Slough. The Hazens had been about ready to turn in for the night. Then . . .

"Petey Franks, he came across the slough from Gull Island in his boat. His woman, Petey said, was bad sick again with the chills and fever misery. Petey wanted to know if I had a quinine bottle and would I come over for a while. My Bid told me to go ahead—that he'd go to bed. So I went with Petey. His woman was pretty bad, all right, plumb out of her head with the fever. It was right close to midnight, I reckon, when I got her finally quieted down. Petey brought me back and then lit out for home again, real quick. I went in to go to bed and—and Bid, he wasn't there."

Mrs. Hazen paused in her low-voiced monologue, and began to shiver and whimper a bit. Molly Profitt poured more coffee. Presently Mrs. Hazen went on.

"I waited a little bit, figuring that maybe Bid had just got restless waiting for me and had gone outside for a time. But then, when he didn't show, I went—went looking for him. I—I found him, up on the levee. I—I bumped right into him. Gave me the most horrible fright ever. For he—he was swinging on the end of a rope under that big oak tree that marks Heron Point. My—

my Bid was hanging there—hanging there. And when I bumped into him he kept swinging—back and forth—back and—forth—and—and—!"

She caught at Molly Profitt and went all to pieces again, wailing and whimpering and crying in a dry and dreadful way.

Molly Profitt looked up with grave intentness. "You've got things to do, Dan Scoville. I'll take care of this poor thing."

"Yeah," nodded Scoville savagely. "Things to do."

He went into the back room, strapped on his gun, got his coat. Tod had followed him in there. Boyish fists were clenched and a boyish chin was quivering with sympathetic grief.

"That—that damn Cole Logan! Just like with my pap—he's done it to Bid Hazen."

"No!" Scoville's tone was the curtest he'd yet used with the boy. "That won't do, Tod. None of that kind of talk unless you're sure. And right now you're not sure who did this thing. Understand? No talk like that. Now you stick around and help Mrs. Profitt all you can."

Then Scoville took the sting out of the rebuke by dropping a hand on the boy's shoulder. "This is an office of the law, Tod. And you're part of it. And the law doesn't make talk just on a guess. It has to be sure before it speaks out. See what I mean, kid?"

"Yeah, I see," admitted the boy, a trifle

grudgingly. “I won’t talk no more. You—you be careful, Dan.”

“Sure, Tod—all the time.”

Bill Profitt followed Dan Scoville out onto the porch.

“Christ!” growled the storekeeper, and there was no profanity in the word, but rather the admission of his own churned-up feelings. “Can you think of a rougher deal than that? That poor woman bumps into her own husband—actually bumps into him, while he’s hanging by his neck—dead! Me, I don’t rile easy, but right now I’m mad enough to raise a sizable chunk of hell for somebody. If only I knew which way to hit. Yeah, she bumps into her own man, hanging there dead. And then she comes all the way to town on foot with the memory riding her—and the fog full of ghosts—! You’ll be needing help, Dan—to cut him down and take care of him. You want me along?”

Scoville shook his head. “No need, Bill. You can do more good here, giving your wife a hand. I’ll get Ed Jethro to ride along with me.”

He dropped down off the porch and went swiftly along to the livery barn. In the harness room there, both Ed Jethro and Sage, the stage driver, were snoring on the two bunks. He woke them, gave them the bleak word.

Ed Jethro broke into a flurry of mumbled curses. “The damned dirty whelps! Now I don’t go along with that sort of miserable business and I don't care who knows it. Be right with you, Dan."

"And here," said Sage, fumbling for his boots. "Three's better than two. All my fault in a way, I guess. I should never have staged Bid Hazen and his missis back to Middle Island."

They rode out of town through that utter blackness which the fog and the early morning laid across the world. Ed Jethro led an extra horse with an empty saddle. They followed along the levee toward Heron Point, and the breath of the slough waters to their left lifted dank and cold.

Dawn came slowly, reluctantly, a gray and creeping thing against the shroud of fog. The slough gave off streamers of chill mist, and reed birds began their first cheeping and a rail set up a harsh cacophony of sound from the depths of a tule patch. The world was coming awake.

In the first substantial steadiness of real daylight they reached Heron Point and the macabre reality of this thing was starkly there before their eyes. The big oak, the rope, and the lank, dangling figure.

They cut Bid Hazen down, and in grim silence rolled the body in a tarp and tied it across the saddle of the spare horse.

"What now, Dan?" asked Sage.

"You and Ed take him back to town," directed

Scoville bleakly. "I'll have a look around and see if I can pick up any sign."

Sage nodded. "Now I wish you luck there, but I doubt you'll have any. This thing's got a wrong look to it somehow. It's just too damn barefaced. Like a piece of danglin' sucker bait. So I'm hoping you won't jump at conclusions, Dan."

Scoville flashed him a quick look. "Meaning what, by that, Sage? What do you know?"

"Don't know a damned thing more than you do," was Sage's enigmatic answer. "Exceptin' this. Was I the real thief, but wanted to make the other feller look like one, then mebbe I'd leave the stolen goods right on his doorstep. All right, Ed—I'm ready if you are."

Sage and Ed Jethro rode away, leading the horse with its dreary burden.

Dan Scoville got out his pipe and puffed at it for some little time while he considered Sage's parting remark. Quite a character, Sage was. A cautious man in some ways, but outspoken in others. And possessed of a deep and discerning shrewdness. He knew Middle Island from end to end, and he knew the people on it. He was the sort, in his dry and listening way, to have an ear always close to the pulse of this land and to recognize and evaluate the currents of thought and action which moved across it. He would, Scoville decided, have to push Sage into a corner one of these days, and really make him talk. Right now, however, there were more immediate and sterner things to think about.

Scoville went down the slope of the levee to the shanty boat, looked it over, and then went inside. It was an old and worn thing, this place of human dwelling, but fairly neat inside. For better or worse, it had been one good woman's world, but one now shattered and broken.

There was no evidence of struggle. Whoever had taken Bid Hazen had evidently surprised him and held him under gun point, then marched him up to the levee crest under the big oak, there to his cruel and ignominious end. There were some boot tracks about the spot of the lynching, but these meant nothing, offered no clue other than it had been a bunch of riding men who had pulled the lynching.

Farther along and down on the south side of the levee there was some fresh horse sign. Here the stranglers had evidently left their mounts, to go in quietly afoot to spring their surprise capture of the luckless shanty-boater.

Scoville spent some time, working over that horse sign. The animals had done considerable restless stamping around and the area was well trampled up. Scoville decided that there had been at least three and perhaps four animals in the group. They had come to this spot by neither the east-running levee along Cross Over Slough nor up from the south along the Ten Mile Slough levee, but straight in from the island proper, and had left across the same wide area. But when he tried to follow this sign, it soon ran out and was lost on tough, springy grassland that held no lasting impression of hoofs.

Convinced that he could do no good here, Scoville headed back for Delta, riding slowly, deep-sunk in grim thought. Here was direct challenge to his ability as a law officer and to the efficiency of his office. If he had been watched and measured before, he would be doubly so now. Here was no mere challenge of his authority by a stubborn, dominant personality like Cole Logan. Here was high crime—murder—and any prestige he'd managed to win among the people of Delta and Middle Island was at stake. He would have to do something concrete about this thing, or he might as well take his star back to Riverton and admit failure to Sheriff Frank Ide.

As he rode, he carefully weighed all that he had experienced and seen and heard since his arrival in Delta. And of all these, two things kept hammering at his consciousness. The first was the day of his arrival in Delta and the first showdown between Cole Logan and himself. How clearly he was recalling some things Cole Logan had said then, after being blocked in his attempt to get his hands on Bid Hazen!

"I can wait. Bid Hazen can't stay in that store

or in this town forever. I'll get my chance to pick him up, and when I do, then he hangs! You got my word on that, law man."

Those were the words Cole Logan had uttered, his exact words. And they had been hammering at him from the moment Mrs. Bid Hazen brought the dread word. And then there was something else. Last night, when Loren Logan had visited him in his office, in explaining how she'd managed to slip away from home alone, she had said something about Cole having gone off in the early night on some sort of errand.

Scoville twisted restlessly in his saddle. What errand? Had it been one to fulfill that spoken threat? Had that lovely, vibrant girl, so fine in her own honesty, unconsciously spoken words that might convict her own brother as a murderer—a strangler?

Scoville's face was harsh and set when he rode into Delta through a mist of fog that was beginning to pale and thin out before the burn of a newly risen sun.

That the word about Bid Hazen was out was plain to see. Men, most of them levee cabin or shanty-boat men, were on the street, moving restlessly about in little groups, talking and arguing. When Scoville pulled up in front of his office, several of them headed that way, and it was George Delbert who led them. Scoville was inside, standing beside his desk table, when they came pushing in. The lawyer challenged Scoville with his bulging eyes.

"Well?" he demanded acidly. "What have you done about this rotten business?"

Scoville surveyed him for a long, cold moment. "I've done a little checking," he said curtly.

"Checking!" growled one of the group with Delbert. "Why waste time piddling around that way? Go gather in them responsible. You know who did it, same as all the rest of us do. What's the matter, Deputy—you afraid to face up to Cole Logan?"

In three quick steps, Dan Scoville had hold of the speaker, and, with a powerful twist of his shoulders, flung the fellow back with a crash against the office wall. As the man bounced away, he ran into a spread hand against his chest and a stiff left arm that drove him into the wall again and held him there.

"Mister," gritted Scoville, "you talk too damn much. When you say I know who lynched Bid Hazen, you lie! When you say you know who did it, you lie again! Or were you there? Did you see Hazen hung? Did you?"

The shanty-boater's chin wobbled and dropped, and his eyes blinked dazedly before the angry, icy stare Scoville put on him. He gulped and stammered.

"Me—me there? Of course not. I was in bed asleep. I—"

“Then you don’t know a damn thing, do you?” cut in Scoville. “Not a damn thing. You were just talking—shooting off your big mouth. That’s dangerous business, mister. So close that mouth of yours before I slap it shut!”

He let go of the fellow and turned on George Delbert, the anger running loose in him, now.

“I don’t know what you think you rate, Delbert. But in my book you’re just a damned cheap shyster. And if you think that gives you the right to come in this office and tell me what to do, you’re badly mistaken. I’ll handle my own office in my own way without any advice from you, now or at any other time. Now get out, the whole lot of you, before I throw you out!”

Delbert’s froggy eyes blinked and blinked as he backed toward the door. There, he seemed to gather a little courage and his voice lifted, thin and pettish.

“As a citizen I’ve the right—”

“Get out!” Scoville started for him.

Delbert stumbled through the door with the others, and Scoville slammed it shut behind them. Then he stood for a moment, bleakly taut. Behind him there was a soft step and he turned to see Tod Neely standing in the doorway of the inner room, eyes round but still clouded a little with sleep.

“After Missis Profitt took Missis Hazen into her place, I turned in again, Dan. Wasn’t nothin’ else I could do. I heard you givin' them fellers what for. If they'd started anything rough with you, I was all ready to pitch in."

Scoville studied Tod for a moment. There was no doubt of the lad's sincerity. Tod was scared, but there was a definite set to his youthful jaw. Some of the tension ran out of Scoville. He smiled.

"Sure you were, Tod—sure you were. You and me—we'll handle them who need it. Now what do you say to some breakfast?"

They went across to Mrs. Tyce's eating house, this tall, lean man and the stripling boy, and there was deep pride in Tod as he half walked, half trotted to keep up.

"You sure handled Joe Mills right, Dan. He was talkin' when he didn't know what he was talkin' about. And he had no right to do that."

Scoville dropped a hand on the boy's shoulder. "You're learning, Tod."

The Block L headquarters was almost like a small village. There were wide, fenced meadows and a sprawling run of corrals. There were feed sheds and barns and a number of clustered cabins. A little to one side and dominating all the rest was a big, square, two-story ranch house, with a wide veranda all across the front of it. Two windmills glinted in the now bright sunshine and spun busily to the push of the ocean-fresh breeze coming in from the west.

Dan Scoville rode directly in toward this, showing no outward sign of the taut wariness within him. This was the heart and center of the Logan power, the very lair of an opposition as unpredictable as it was strange.

There were several men in sight about the corrals and feed sheds and barns, and behind one of the cabins a woman was hanging out an early-morning wash. When Scoville drew closer, there was a stir about the place and then there was a man moving out on foot to face him. It was Duff Twining.

Twining's leathery face was harsh, his eyes unreadable. His voice was curtly low.

"You're a nervy fool, Scoville. Don't you realize you're pushing your luck, showing up here?"

Scoville shrugged. "Sometimes a man's got to do that, Twining. I got some business with Cole Logan, and how else would I see him? Where is he?"

"Around," admitted Twining briefly. "What is this business?"

Dan Scoville did not answer right away. Instead he let his glance swing. Over at the corner of a feed shed was the hulking, unmistakable figure of Waco Dart, watching intently. There were other riders in similar positions of vantage. Scoville brought his glance back to Duff Twining.

"Anybody," he said, "would think I was a

damned army, instead of a lone man with a star. What's the matter with this layout? Got a guilty conscience, maybe?"

"Nothing wrong with my conscience," retorted Duff Twining. "What do you want to see Cole about?"

"An important item of business," Scoville told him curtly. "A dead man. A dead man hanging on the end of a rope. A man named Bid Hazen!"

Watching closely as he said this, Dan Scoville saw that there was no mistaking the start of honest surprise which showed in Duff Twining's eyes. It wasn't faked.

"The hell!" Twining exploded. "You mean—somebody lynched Hazen?"

"No less," rapped Scoville. "Last night. Sometime around midnight. You sleep good last night, Twining?"

"Yeah," answered Twining quietly, his words as straight and unwavering as his glance. "Yeah, I did. And as far as I know, so did everybody else on this ranch. Get me right. If I said I was heartbroken at the news, I'd be lying. You know how I feel about Bid Hazen and all of his stripe. But Block L had nothing to do with lynching him."

"I want to hear what Cole Logan has to say about that," Scoville insisted. "Where is he?"

Cole Logan answered this question by appearing on the veranda of the big ranch house.

His heavy voice boomed across the interval. "What is this, Duff? What does that deputy want?"

Twining turned toward the ranch house with a shrug. "Come on, Scoville."

Scoville dismounted and walked along with Duff Twining, leading the claybank gelding. Coming up to the ranch house, it seemed he could sense a difference in Cole Logan. Cole was still a big, dark, dominating figure and, while the old truculence was there, it was under control, somehow. There was more of a settled stillness in the man, instead of that old, wild, headlong imperiousness. As his glance held that of Scoville's at close range, he spoke growlingly.

"You must know you're not welcome here. What are you trying to do, lay on the pressure?"

"That," answered Scoville, "is a thought that never even occurred to me. But I got some questions to ask you, so I figured to ride in and ask them. What do you know about the lynching of Bid Hazen?"

As it had been with Duff Twining, Scoville saw a start of pure surprise flame in Cole's eyes. "You mean Bid Hazen—was lynched? Hell! That's news to me. Good news, I might add. But still—news."

There was a stir at the ranch-house door and then it was Loren Logan who stood there. She looked strangely young and girlish. She was in blue-and-white-checked gingham and her hair was drawn back in a heavy braid which fell between her shoulders. Her gray eyes were sober and full of concern. Scoville inclined his head, touched his hat. Her words came out at him, anxious and disturbed.

"Did—did I hear you say that—that Bid Hazen had been lynched, Mr. Scoville?"

"That's right," Scoville told her. "Last night. Somewhere around midnight or a little before. His wife had been out to tend to an ailing neighbor. Hazen was supposed to have been in bed. When his wife came home he wasn't there. She went looking for him and bumped into him in the dark. He was hanging to a tree."

Scoville saw her catch her breath and her eyes go big and dark with distress. "How—how ghastly!" she cried softly. "And you think we—Cole—our men are responsible?"

Cole turned on Scoville savagely before he could answer. "Did you have to throw that kind of picture right in Loren's face? Scoville, you don't know what you're asking for. There's a limit to my patience."

"And mine," shot back Scoville. "Last night a man was lynched, murdered is a better word. I'm out to find the answers. And I'm going to find them, no matter where I have to look for them." He turned to Loren again. "I think you wanted the truth, didn't you?"

She had her hands pressed together in front of her, as she stood rigid and sapling straight. "Of—of course. But surely you didn't think you'd find the answer to that—that lynching here?"

Instead of answering her, Scoville looked at Cole Logan again. "The day I first hit Delta—and kept you off Bid Hazen's back—you made your talk, Logan. You said then that sooner or later you'd come up with Hazen again, and that when you did he'd hang. Correct me if I'm wrong," he added dryly.

Cole got that badgered bear look about him again. "All right—I made that threat. And I'm not saying I wouldn't have made good on it, too. But I haven't laid eyes on Hazen since that day. You can believe that or not, as you please. But it's the truth. Do you believe me?"

Instead of answering the question, Scoville shot another of his own. "Did you stay in last night from dark on, or did you do any riding at all?" Scoville felt a tautness creeping up in him as he asked this. I wonder, he thought, if you'll answer that straight. For you did do some riding. I know you did, because your own sister told me so.

"Why, yes," said Cole bluntly. "I did do some riding. One of my men reported last evening that a couple of shanty boats had tied up along Back Slough—that's the slough at the south end of the island. I got some cattle down that way, and I wondered if maybe those shanty-boaters didn't have some ideas about some fresh beef. So I rode down to Back Slough and patrolled the levee there for three or four hours. I'd say it was around eleven o'clock when I got home and turned in. Do you believe me?" Cole was insistent on this point.

Scoville nodded slowly. "Yes, I believe you. I just wanted to hear you say it. Now, you've spoken for yourself. How about your crew? You got a big one."

At Scoville's elbow, Duff Twining spoke, growling. "I answered for the crew. Do you believe me?"

Scoville nodded again. "Strange as it may seem to some, yes, I do. Strange, because of all the things I've heard about this outfit and its ways. Strange, because of what I've seen with my own eyes and heard with my own ears. Like what you and Waco Dart were set to do to Hazen, back at the Spanish Slough ferry, and because of what's already happened between me and the Logan layout. Yet, I believe you, because I think that all the way through, with maybe one or two exceptions, you're just too damned stiff-necked an outfit to take refuge behind a lie of that sort. It would be more like you, if you had done it, to admit it openly and then ask the rest of the world just what they proposed to do about it. Yet I had to ride out and get your answer in your own words."

"Well, you've had it," rapped Cole. "And now you know the way back to town."

Scoville looked at Cole, a slow and bitter anger beginning to burn in him. He had conducted this thing fairly and squarely. He had asked only questions he felt had to be asked, and he had accepted Logan's and Duff Twining's word at face value. He had hoped that this fact would break down some barriers and bring about a more friendly and co-operative attitude. But the hope apparently was an empty one. His voice rang harshly.

"You sure are one hospitable hombre, Logan. I treat you fair, yet you would treat me like some damned scavenger. I'll remind you that I could have been plenty nasty about this thing. On the basis of threats you've made and what a lot of people think of you, I could have slapped an arrest on you and hauled you out to Riverton to stand trial for the murder of Hazen. I might not have cinched you, but I sure as hell could have made it hot for you. Now I'll tell you that I've made my last bid for your friendship."

Without waiting for an answer, Scoville turned away and swung into his saddle. Anger boiled higher in him every moment, anger at the stubborn, implacable hostility of Cole Logan. The man might have toned down some from the heights of his self-assumed authority, but that was all.

He knew that Logan and Twining had given him

the truth regarding Bid Hazen. Their surprise at the news he'd given them had been real and convincing. There had been no hedging, no evasiveness in their answers. The guilt for Hazen's murder did not lay at this headquarters.

He had made a lot of concessions, figuratively, to bring about some sort of amicable understanding between himself and Cole Logan, knowing that such an understanding was highly desirable as far as his official standing on Middle Island was concerned. Achieved, it would have had its effect the length and breadth of the island and of the country round about. But there was just no way of making Cole Logan understand that, it seemed. The man was just plain too damn stiff-necked.

Dan Scoville wanted to look back, to have another look at that slim figure in gingham, who had seemed as fresh and cool as the morning itself. But he was through making overtures to any Logan, he told himself, savagely. He'd show this Logan outfit he could be just as stiff-necked as they were, only more so.

He knew a lot of eyes were watching him leave, but he kept his own glance straight ahead. The devil take the whole lot of them. . . .

Behind him, Cole Logan's voice suddenly erupted in a harsh shout.

"Rack—put that gun down! Rack—damn you—!"

To Dan Scoville, it was as though he had ridden straight into the very center of a lightning bolt. There was the wild thunder, the jagged, blinding flash of light, the massive impact. Then he was falling into endless blackness. . . .

IX—Store Boat

The blackness left him slowly. It was like crawling up out of some dark pit, inch by inch. He became aware of pain, a steady, pounding pain in his head. And sound, which had been a small, run-together hodgepodge, slowly steadied into distinct parts. It took an amazing amount of will and effort to get his eyes open, but he managed it.

For a moment he thought he must be awakening from a bad dream, and that he lay back on his bunk in the office at Delta. But as he explored things with his numbed and aching senses he knew better. He was in a wide bed and between sheets and this room was a strange one. He rolled his head for a better look around and only partly bit back the groan of savage pain which this move set up in his tortured skull.

There was a stir of movement and a woman leaned over him. A middle-aged woman whom he'd never seen before, plain of face, but with kind eyes.

"You mustn't try and move," she warned him quietly. "Drink this."

She held a glass to his lips. What he drank tasted bitter, but it was wet and good and seemed to cool him all the way through. He closed his eyes and tried to figure this thing out. Before he got very far toward an answer, he fell asleep.

There was subdued lamplight in the room when he woke. He felt better, just a hell of a lot better. That murderous, throbbing pound in his head had subsided to a dull ache. He heard the murmur of voices and he cleared his throat and mumbled, "All right. Just where am I, anyhow?"

The powerful figure of Cole Logan moved up beside the bed. "Temporary guest of the Logans," was the growled answer. "How you feeling?"

"Good enough. What happened?"

A gust of dark shadow swept across Cole's face. "Rack. You were riding out when he threw a gun and cut down on you. Barely clipped you across the head. The biggest quarter of an inch you'll ever know was the difference between the way you are now, or bcing laid out for burying."

"Nice fellow, Rack!" murmured Scoville.

"It was a damned dirty trick," said Cole harshly. "I hope you don't think it was anybody else's idea except Rack's?"

Scoville met Cole's brooding glance. "No," he said. "I don't. How long have I been here?"

"Since yesterday. Anything you want?"

"Could stand a mite of grub. A cup of coffee would help a lot. Yeah, a little food, and my clothes. Then I'll take myself off your hands."

Cole shook his head. "You won't be leaving today. Tomorrow, maybe, if you're up to it. I'll have that food brought in."

Cole tramped out and Scoville was alone for a little time. He ran an exploring hand across his head, encountered a cap of bandage. He wagged his head from side to side, raised and lowered it. It took a little effort to do this and a warning stab of pain made him blink his eyes. So he was quickly content to lie still.

Two feminine figures came into the room. Nora Baine and Loren Logan. Loren carried a tray, which gave off the welcome aroma of steaming coffee. Nora Baine smiled down at him.

"Can you sit up and eat, or do you have to be fed? We'll stand no contrariness, understand."

"Don't want to be treated like an infant," he grumbled. "Maybe if you'd stack some pillows behind me—"

They did this, Nora supporting his head while Loren tucked pillows under his shoulders and head. He set his teeth and squinted his eyes, but as soon as he was steady his head quieted again. As she worked over him, Loren's face was but inches from his own, and her gray eyes were like deep, soft, limpid pools. He saw the soft flush steal up her throat and she turned away, busy with the tray.

The coffee was good and so were the soft-boiled egg and toast. He licked up the last crumb, sighed. "Thanks," he said simply. "Now if I only had my pipe—"

It was Nora Baine who located this and packed

it for him. Loren Logan went out, carrying the empty tray. Nora leaned swiftly down and brushed her lips against his cheek.

"That," she said, a little tremor in her voice, "for what you didn't do along the trail after you'd left our house the other day. Loren has told me all about it. How Cole threw a gun—and missed, praise heaven! And how you could have shot in return, but didn't. I'll bless you forever for that, Dan Scoville."

Loren came back, carrying a glass. Scoville looked at it with distrust. "Is that some more of that bitter as blazes stuff?"

"It is," she said calmly. "And you're going to drink it. Here!"

He took the glass meekly, but managed to press her hand as he did so. She flushed again, but met his eyes and held them steadily.

"For that," she said tartly, "you can reflect on your sins alone. Come along, Nora."

They went out, and for a time Scoville sucked on his pipe. By the time it went dead, a great drowsiness settled over him again, and he put the pipe aside, slid down on his pillows, and went off to sleep again.

The cool light of morning filled the room when again he awoke. Loren Logan stood alone beside his bed, holding a breakfast tray. She stood for some time in silence, looking down at him gravely. Finally she spoke.

"If you feel up to it, Cole said you can leave today."

Scoville grinned and yawned. "Feel like I'd slept for a week. And I'm good as new. I'll be traveling. I been a bother long enough."

She shook her head. "It hasn't been that at all—a bother, I mean. We've done little enough for you, considering what Rack did. I—I hope you don't feel that Cole intended anything like that?"

"Not at all," said Scoville emphatically. "I told Cole I didn't. Now that I'm remembering clearly, I recall hearing Cole yell at Rack just before the lightning hit. Maybe I really should thank Rack. For he gave me this chance to see you and speak to you like this. You are, you know," he added softly, "very lovely to look at and speak to, Loren."

She colored hotly and tossed her head. "I don't believe I like flip talk."

"I'm not trying to be flip," protested Scoville. "I never meant anything more in my life. I want you to believe that."

Again she studied him with grave eyes. Then she said quietly, "Very well—you weren't being flip. Now eat your breakfast."

It was a hearty one and Scoville took care of it with gusto. While he did so, Loren moved quietly about the room, tidying up things which were already tidy. Watching her guardedly, Scoville sensed that she had something on her mind which was troubling her. A moment later he knew what it was, for she came over to the side of the bed and sat there.

"When you leave here, you'll be searching further for whoever it was that did that—that awful thing to Bid Hazen?"

Scoville nodded. "Yes, I will. Frankly, though, I don't know where to look. Why do you ask?"

She stared at the bedcovers, plucking at them with her fingers. "This may mean something—or nothing. I—I wouldn't want to accuse any innocent person. But I've been thinking of something—"

"Thinking is not accusing, Loren. What is it?"

Her head came up and she looked at him steadily. "The other night—that foggy one—when I was on my way home after visiting you in your office—the night Bid Hazen was—was lynched, well, some riders passed me along the trail. They didn't see me or know I was there, for I heard them in time to get well out of the way and the night was so dark and the fog so thick, they had no idea I was anywhere near. Anyhow, as they passed, I heard one of them make a remark. At the time, I didn't give it a second thought. But now, in the light of what happened that night, maybe—"

"What was the remark, Loren?" Scoville was grave and intent, now.

"I can't recall the exact words, but it was something about the fog being some good, anyhow, and that it would be a help on a job of this kind."

Scoville's eyes pinched thoughtfully. "It was a good night for murder. And for that sort of business, the fog would help. Girl, I wish you could have identified that speaker!"

"Maybe I can," was her startling reply. "His voice was very hoarse and—well, sort of—of gravelly, if you understand what I mean. I heard that voice before, one day in town. I was in Bill Profitt's store, when this man came in to buy something. I remember thinking then that it was about as harsh a human voice as I'd ever heard. I don't know his last name, but I heard Bill Profitt call him Jake. He—he rides for Ward Requa!"

For a long moment Dan Scoville was absolutely still, his glance fixed on the empty space of speculation. Then he spoke softly. "It ties in! It ties in with things I've been wondering about, things I've tried to figure, but couldn't make hard sense of—until now. Yeah—it ties in!"

He reached out, caught her startled hand, held it warmly. He smiled. "Girl, you're wonderful! You're not only lovely enough to turn a man's head and heart upside down—but you're smart. Yeah, you're wonderful."

A soft confusion held her and that warm color was a swift beating glory in her cheeks. Her eyes grew very big, as she stared at him, wordless. Then she had tugged her hand free and was halfway across the room, like a startled bird.

"You—you shouldn't say those things to me," she stammered.

"Why not—when I mean them—mean every word?"

She caught up the empty tray and would have hurried out, but Scoville's plea stopped her at the door. "Please, Loren—you haven't said anything about what you heard along the trail to anyone else, have you?"

She looked at him over her shoulder. "No. Only to you."

"Good! Don't tell anyone else. Not to Cole, or anyone. Promise?"

"I promise."

"Good girl! And, Loren, even if I were going to be shot for it, I've still got to say that you're lovely."

Some of her confusion left her and in its place came the glimmer of a smile that became a soft laugh. "That kind of talk from a hard-boiled man of the law! You're well again, all right. I'll send Aunt Ella in to have another look at that head of yours. Then you're free to go. Your clothes are on that chair yonder."

Aunt Ella was the kindly-eyed woman who had been the first person he saw after recovering consciousness. She worked deftly, taking off the cap of bandage and replacing it with a new and smaller one.

"You are not only hardheaded, but you heal very quickly," she said. "And you are lucky, young man—in more ways than one."

She was gone before Scoville could get her to amplify on this last puzzling statement.

He was a little groggy when he got out of bed and reached for his clothes. But by the time he was dressed he was steady enough and, aside from a slightly gone feeling under his ribs, felt just about as good as ever. His head, though sore, was clear and quiet. Now came further steps at the door of the room and it was harsh-faced Duff Twining who came in.

"I was supposed to help you get into those duds," Twining said. "But it looks like you don't need me. In a lot of ways you're a tough hombre, Scoville."

Scoville grinned crookedly. "This is a world of tough hombres, Duff. Like yourself, for instance. So, to get along in it, I have to try and hold up my end. Where's Cole? I want to thank him for his hospitality."

Twining did not answer, just shrugged and led the way down a flight of stairs and out of a side door, where two mounts stood saddled and ground tied. One of these was Scoville's claybank gelding. His gun belt and holstered six-shooter hung from the saddle horn. As he buckled on the weapon, Scoville looked around.

"Others I'd like to thank," he said.

"She ain't here," commented Twining dryly. "She left a little bit ago to visit with Nora Baine. Come on—let's go."

Scoville flashed him a quick glance. "I'm heading for town. Where are you going?"

"Down the trail a piece with you."

"That," drawled Scoville, "has all the earmarks of me being escorted off Logan property. Maybe with instructions not to come back?"

Duff Twining shook his head. "Not exactly."

Duff had a rifle slung in a scabbard under his stirrup leather. When they had gone a little way, Scoville pointed to the weapon. "What's the idea of that? New addition since I last saw you in a saddle."

Twining spun up a brown paper cigarette. "Rack's on the loose," he said bluntly. "And that's where Cole is, trying to locate him. You made a bad mistake, Scoville, when you gun-whipped Rack. You should either have left him completely alone, or finished him. For he'll never rest now until he gets you. He came damned close, day before yesterday."

Scoville shrugged. "Reckon I can stand up under the strain of waiting. Tell me this. Did Cole and Rack have a showdown after Rack took that cut at me?"

"Did they?" Duff swore for emphasis. "Hell—

I'll say they did! I thought for a time there they were going to shoot it out. And that would have been very bad, for Cole's slow and awkward with a gun, while Rack's poison that way. Anyhow, Cole really peeled the hide off him. I've seen something of the sort coming for a long time. Your stepping into the picture just sort of hurried it along.

"Yeah, Cole sure laid it on the line to Rack. So, sometime during last night, Rack pulled out. Don't know where he went. Nobody does. But wherever he is, you can bet he's cooking up some kind of hell for somebody. For Rack's renegade stuff. He hates easy and he's vengeful as hell. Which Cole well knows. So he's out, with some of the boys, trying to locate Rack."

"Strange that Cole never settled with Rack before."

Duff shrugged. "Rack's got Logan blood in him, and Cole will remember that as long as he can. He's stood for a lot from Rack in the past, but this time it's different."

Scoville glanced at Duff's rifle again, then spoke dryly. "You, I suppose, had orders to see that I got safe back to town?"

Twining nodded. "That's about right."

"A change in Logan tactics," Scoville murmured. "Not so very long ago, all the Block L outfit was hot after my scalp."

"One of them still is. Rack. Don't forget that."

Taking a final deep drag on his cigarette, Duff Twining crushed the butt to crumbs on his saddle horn. "Cole—he's changed. Ain't sure just why. But all of a sudden he's got a different slant on things. I shouldn't wonder, if your luck holds out, if you and Cole don't end up on pretty fair terms."

"Now that," said Scoville quickly, "is sure the way I hope things turn out." Then he added, grinning, "After snarling and yelling and roaring at each other, and doing our damnedest best to beat the other fellow's brains out, we get to be friends. Man is a damn funny animal, Duff."

Duff showed a small grin in return. "Ain't he though! After the way you handled me at the Spanish Slough ferry, I thought I'd never be happy again until I'd seen your hide hung up to dry. Now I figure that you and me can probably live in the same county without trying to claw each other to pieces." Duff cleared his throat harshly. "Which way you going to look in that Bid Hazen affair, now you're reasonable convinced that Block L didn't have anything to do with it?"

"Any way and all ways," answered Scoville guardedly. "You got any suggestions?"

Duff Twining considered this for a moment in silence. Then with slow gravity, he said, "Making charges is easy, but proving them is something else again. I'll say this. There's them who hate the everlasting Logan guts. They're afraid to take it out on the Logans direct, but if they could finagle the Block L into some kind of a jackpot that would bust Block L power complete on Middle Island, that would suit them just fine. I ain't naming any names, but if you look around long and shrewd enough, you'll probably get some idea of what I'm driving at. It's something for you to think on, anyway."

A mile from Delta, Duff Twining turned back, and Dan Scoville rode the balance of the distance alone. Surveying town as he came up to it, Scoville saw, lifting above the levee, the top hamper of a sizable river boat, tied up at the Delta wharf. He saw also, as he turned into the street, quite a few people in evidence. Evidently, he thought, the presence of the boat must be an event of some importance.

As Scoville pulled to a halt at the stable, Ed Jethro and Sage came out, leading a pair of saddle broncs. Sage exclaimed in profane relief.

"Time you were showing up. Where in hell you been? Ed and me were just about to start ridin' and lookin' for you."

Scoville smiled briefly as he dismounted. "Nice to know I've been missed. What's going on, Sage? Why all the people in town?"

"Couple of reasons. Pitch Branner's got his store boat tied up at the wharf. Whenever the

Island Queen shows up, that always brings people out. Then that fool windbag of a George Delbert has been yappin' up and down, screaming for justice in Bid Hazen's lynching. And he's got a flock of shanty-boat men all worked up and following him around like a flock of damn-fool geese. You better knock Delbert's ears back, Dan. Give him time to talk enough, that man could be dangerous. What happened to your head?"

"Bumped it."

"And managed that fancy bandage all by yourself, I suppose?" snorted Sage. "Like hell! You been missing too long and you got a little bit of a peaked look to you. What's the real story?"

"That can wait. But I sure do appreciate you and Ed worrying about me."

"Ed and me and others," growled Sage. "Tod Neely and Molly Profitt have been throwing fits. You better get over to your office and cool them down. Ed and me'll take care of the claybank."

The office door was open and Scoville went in quietly. But youthful ears are sharp ears, and Tod Neely came charging in from the inner room, grabbing at Scoville.

"Dan—Dan! Where you been?"

Scoville wrapped a comforting arm about the lad's shoulders. "Got held up a little, Tod. But everything's all right."

Tod wasn't holding anything back. All the open honesty of boyhood's feelings was in the way he clung to Scoville. He whimpered a little, and when he finally pulled away, he scrubbed the back of a brown fist across his eyes.

"From now on, when you go anywhere, Dan—I'm going with you. You've been hurt. Your head's tied up."

Scoville smiled down at him. "Fellow gets jimmed up now and then, Tod. Tell you all about it, later. I hear Mrs. Profitt's been worrying some. You go tell her I'm all right."

At the doorway the boy paused. "You find out who—who lynched Bid Hazen, Dan?"

"Not yet, Tod. But I will. Things like that take a little time."

Tod went on his way, and Scoville dropped into a chair, annoyed with himself because his legs felt a mite shaky. Damned strange how a little clip on the head could drag a man down so. There was a flurry of steps on the porch and Molly Profitt came in.

"Dan Scoville," she scolded gently, "you'll be the death of Tod and me yet—worrying us so. Tod says you've been hurt. Here, look at me!"

She studied Scoville's face intently, then nodded to herself. "There's a seediness in you yet. I don't know what happened to your head. I know that in your own good time you'll tell about that. But of this I'm sure. You're not fit for too much activity just yet. You go on in and lie down."

The idea wasn't at all objectionable to Scoville. His head had begun to throb a little. He smiled as he hauled himself to his feet.

"Your wisdom, ma'am, is only exceeded by the size of your heart."

He went into the back room and flattened out on his bunk, and the weakness that was in him lured sleep before he knew it.

It was midafternoon when he awoke to the sound of voices in the front office. Just now it was Tod Neely who was speaking.

"I'm sorry, Mister Requa. But right now Dan's sleepin', and Missis Profitt, she said he needed it. So I ain't waking him up for nobody."

Scoville swung his feet off the bunk and stood up. He had the welcome feeling of increasing soundness all through him. That added sleep seemed to have really brought him over the hump. He went into the front office. Ward Requa showed his cynical grin.

"You ought to rake up another star and pin it on this kid, Scoville. He's a hard customer to try and convince."

Tod looked a little sheepish. "I was just making sure that you had your sleep out, Dan."

Scoville rumpled the lad's hair. "Best darn assistant deputy in the country. Obliged, Tod. Now you can run along. I'll hold down the fort."

The boy, with some chestiness, trotted out.

Scoville took a chair, got out his pipe. "What's on your mind, Requa?"

"Curiosity, mainly. Things seem to be stewing about that Hazen affair. Cabin men and shanty-boaters, so I hear, are about to band together, bust loose, and do something."

"So—o! Do what?"

"Go after them responsible for the Hazen lynching."

"Then they know who did it, eh? Well, that's more than I do."

"They know who's done that sort of thing in the past. So they can make a pretty fair guess."

Scoville ran a match across the bowl of his pipe, puffed for a moment in silence. Then he said, with some crispness, "I doubt they'll get very far. And guessing, in a matter of this sort, just won't do."

Requa shrugged. "Can't blame 'em for being worked up. What happened to your head?"

"Rack Logan took a shot at me."

"The hell! You must have been tramping on the Logan tail pretty hard."

"I'd been asking a few questions," admitted Scoville. "But that wasn't what set Rack off. His grudge is a private one."

"Because of that gun-whipping you gave him?"

Scoville nodded. "I reckon. Mostly that, anyway."

Requa shrugged again. "You sure insist on learning things the hard way, my friend. As I recall, I warned you of something like this. I told you you'd made a bad mistake in buffaloing Rack instead of finishing him when you had the chance. Did you have any better luck this time at Rack than he had at you?"

"Hell, no! My light went out too quick. I didn't even hear the shot. The world just came apart all of a sudden. Next thing I knew I was in bed in the Logan ranch house with a bandage on my head. Pretty nice people, most of the Logans are, once you get to know them."

Ward Requa twisted up a cigarette with meticulous care. "Nothing like spreading a little honey to cover up a trail."

"What trail, Requa?"

"Why the trail from where Bid Hazen was left, dangling at the end of a rope."

The glance Scoville laid on Requa was level and intent. "You got any proof to back up that kind of talk? If you haven't, don't make it."

"I know this," retorted Requa. "I know that a wolf don't change into an amiable sheep dog overnight."

"And I know," said Scoville curtly, "that the Block L had nothing to do with Bid Hazen's death."

"How do you know? You mentioned proof a minute ago. What's your proof there?"

"Among other things, Cole Logan's word for it."

Ward Requa got to his feet, dragging deep on his cigarette. "I will be damned!" he said softly. "I can't figure you, Scoville. I don't know whether you're blind, or sheep dumb—or both. Here Cole Logan throws his weight all over you, damn near beats you to death with his fists. Rack Logan tries to blow your head off. Which should be enough, it seems to me, to convince any man how the Logan mind and methods work. Yet you stand willing to take the Logan word as being gospel. You beat me—you surely do!"

Requa went out the door, flipping his cigarette butt ahead of him.

Dan Scoville sat for a time, smoking, his face furrowed with thought. Then he got up and went out on the porch. Farther along, Tod Neely was industriously sweeping the area in front of Bill Profitt's store. Scoville called softly, "Tod!" then beckoned as the boy looked up. Tod put aside his broom and came at a barefoot trot.

"Something you wanted, Dan?"

"Yes. Ward Requa just left here. Wonder could you keep an eye on him while he's in town? See where he goes and what he does and who he talks to. Don't let on what you're doing, Tod—and don't say a word to anybody. I'll be waiting in the office to hear about it."

Tod's eyes grew big and took on an excited shine. "Golly, Dan! Do you figure—?"

"We'll see, Tod. You run along and start looking."

It was a half hour before Tod came scurrying in again, and just before he did so Scoville, watching through the open door, saw Requa jog past on his way out of town.

Tod showed mixed emotions. "Guess I didn't do too well, Dan. All I saw was Requa talking to George Delbert in the Wagon Wheel. I couldn't go inside, of course, but I had a good look through the window in front. And all I saw was Requa and Delbert at the bar, drinking and talking. So I hung around until Requa came out and got his horse. Delbert came that far with him, and I heard Requa say one thing that didn't make sense to me."

Scoville, listening intently to the boy's report, asked, "What did you hear him say, Tod?"

"Why, I heard him say to Delbert, 'He's too damn dumb to know his own hand in front of his face.' Sorry I didn't find out something worthwhile, Dan."

Scoville stared out the open door, his eyes squinted, a half smile on his lips. "You found out more than you realize, Tod. You did swell. Now what do you say to you and me going up to have a look at that store boat tied at the wharf?"

At close survey, Pitch Branner's store boat,

the *Island Queen*, was dirty and weather-beaten, with scabbed and peeling paint, foul bottom, rusty stack, and with brasswork green from long lack of polish. The short foredeck was cluttered and untidy, and a couple of shiftless-looking deck hands lounged there. Several of the boat's windows were broken out and rolled-up gunny sacks wadded into the breaks. Near the waist of the craft a closed cargo door was outlined with grime, and from the sill, slimy streaks spread down to the water line. About these streaks, flies buzzed and clustered.

Standing on the end of the wharf, Dan Scoville nursed his pipe and watched the people straggling back and forth across the rickety gangplank. Most of these were cabin men and shanty-boaters, some of them accompanied by their drab-looking women, carrying a few frugal purchases.

Tod Neely, restless at Dan Scoville's side, said, "You figuring on buying anything, Dan—you better do it now. Pitch Branner ain't staying here overnight. This morning I heard him tell a man that he aimed to work on the evening tide up as far as Pike's Landing."

Scoville shook his head, his eyes still fixed on that closed cargo door and the slimy streaks running down from it about which the flies clustered.

"Anything we ever want to buy, Tod—we'll get

at Bill Profitt's store. For he's our good friend. How far is this Pike's Landing?"

"About three miles upslough, on the Gull Island side. Why?"

"Just wondering. Your boat still all right?"

"You bet! Want to see it?"

Tod led the way to the levee end of the wharf, pointed down the sloping bank. The skiff tied up there was ancient and battered, but was dry.

"Looks big enough to haul the two of us, all right," said Scoville. "That ride you've been talking to me about—maybe we'll take it tonight. But mum's the word, Tod. Now you better get back and finish sweeping Bill Profitt's porch."

An hour before sundown, Pitch Branner, in company with several shanty-boat men, dropped down into town and went into the Wagon Wheel. From the door of his office, Dan Scoville watched this group and their destination. A little later he saw the pompous striding figure of George Delbert also turn in at the Wagon Wheel. Scoville waited a few minutes, then headed for the saloon.

Pitch Branner and the rest were lined up at the bar, and their talk frittered out when Scoville came in. But only for a moment. Then Pitch Branner, a burly man with a pouchy, whiskey-veined face, spoke with a heavy heartiness.

"Well now, is that a star I see? It surely is and fine business, too. Good thing for the country, some real law for a change. Means a square deal for the little man."

Maze Dickson, standing at Branner's elbow, muttered, "Just the same kind of square deal Bid Hazen got. A lynch rope around the neck."

Pitch Branner seemed not to hear. Still watching Scoville, he jerked his head. "A drink, friend? I'm buyin'."

Scoville nodded. "Why, thanks. I'll have a short one with you."

In the middle of the group, George Delbert spoke up. "Among others, Scoville—these men here want to know what you intend to do about Bid Hazen's murder?"

Scoville stared hard at the lawyer. "Round up those responsible, of course. Believe I told you that, before."

"Maybe," said Delbert, "some of us are beginning to wonder just how hard you're trying."

"Yeah," seconded Maze Dickson. "Wondering."

"Lay off—lay off!" growled Pitch Branner. "We're here for a friendly drink. Give this law man a chance, can't you? Takes time to round up the guilty, sometimes. Can't expect a law man to go out and tap the first man he sees on the shoulder and say, you're it! Right, Deputy?"

"Right!" drawled Scoville evenly, lifting his glass. "Here's luck!"

Scoville rang some coins on the bar. "Another round," he ordered. "This one on me."

When they had put the second drink away, Scoville let his glance run from man to man. "Heard some talk that you fellows were going to organize, raise hell, and put a rock under it. Just telling you not to try any of that sort of business. I'll handle this matter my own way—and I'll get results. You in particular, Delbert—better chew on that."

They were silent when he walked out.

X—Slough Waters

It was a ghostly world that the skiff slid through. At the start, Tod had insisted he take the oars and he handled these with surprising deftness. But after a bit, Scoville took the lad's place and drove the skiff along with even, unhurried strokes.

Starshine glinted on the slough waters, but threw a light that was tricky and deceiving and, mixed in with the early night mists that were beginning to rise and coil, made a man wonder whether he saw things really, or just imagined he did.

They'd had supper with the Profitts, he and Tod had, a surprise invitation which Molly Profitt had insisted upon and during which Scoville had had to tell the story of his absence and his bandaged head. In return, he'd heard how Bid Hazen had been buried and how Mrs. Hazen had gone out by next morning's stage to live with a sister, back up in a little mining camp in the Sierras.

Both Bill and Molly Profitt had seemed satisfied with Scoville's conclusion that the Block L had had nothing to do with Bid Hazen's lynching.

"If Cole gave you his word on it, that's that," Bill Profitt had declared. "Cole's got his faults, but his word in an affair like that, is good. He's got too much stiff-necked pride to try and hide behind a lie. If he had of hung Bid Hazen, he'd have done it because he figured it the right thing to do, and then he'd have stood up and told the whole cussed world about it."

To which Dan Scoville had agreed. "That's exactly the way I figured it, Bill."

"That Rack, though," Molly Profitt had flared, "he's completely no good. It was like him, to try and shoot you when you weren't looking, Dan."

While they'd been eating, they heard the *Island Queen* pull out, heard the briefly raucous shout of the whistle and then the measured chuffing of exhaust and beat of the paddle wheel as the craft headed east along Cross Over Slough. Now, Dan Scoville was driving Tod Neely's skiff along the same waters and in the same direction.

The slough waters had their night as well as day life. There were rustlings in the tule clumps, where levee and water met. There were squeakings and faint splashings. An owl on the hunt was a flickering phantom close overhead, more sensed than seen on its silent, drifting wings. A little later, from a perch on a tree on the levee, its hooting was a round and hollow booming across the lonely night. Invisible wings made a sibilant rushing across the sky as a wisp of snipe or plover went their mysterious way, come and gone in the space of a breath or two. And once there was a frantic, scrambling splashing close ahead as a brace of startled mud hens beat their clumsy, fumbling departure.

"Just where we heading anyway, Dan?" asked Tod from the skiff's stern.

"Pike's Landing," Scoville told him.

"That's where the *Island Queen*'ll be tied up."

"And that's why we're going there."

"But what do we want with the *Queen*?" asked the puzzled boy. "She was tied up all day at town. And you said that if we wanted to buy anything, we'd buy it at Bill Profitt's store. You didn't seem much interested in the *Queen* at all."

Scoville chuckled softly. "Didn't I, Tod? Well, that's fine. If you didn't think I was interested, then nobody else would. But I was. I noticed some things about the *Queen* that I want a closer look at, without Pitch Branner knowing about it. You keep a sharp lookout, and when we get close to the *Queen* we want to be as quiet as we can."

Scoville angled the skiff in toward the Gull Island side of the slough, which was the north side. Here, where the levee threw dark shadow, he worked his way along with ever-increasing care. The tide was full, almost at the turn. Night, and the weird mixture of utter blackness here and pale star shadow there, gave a man a strange feeling of formlessness, the impression that while he was lending effort to the oars, he really wasn't going anywhere at all.

But Dan Scoville, aside from the serious

business he was on, found a strange and satisfying enjoyment in it all. The wide night laid a deep peacefulness in a man, a sense of freedom. There was a lure to such surroundings as these that stirred up something elemental in a man, and when the invisible rush of plover slushed by overhead, it was easy to let the spirit soar with them. Yes, there was a spell to this kind of country that could get hold of a man and draw him to it.

The magic of the night had hold of the boy, too, apparently, for he was silent with his own thoughts. And so they moved on and on, the measured lift and dip and drive of the oars creating only a soft gurgling, to blend with the faint lipping of the water under the prow of the skiff. Close at hand, and outlined against the stars, the levee crest was a constantly changing thing, ragged with tules one moment, then dipping to flatness for a time until more tules lifted.

Abruptly Tod stirred and then, in a low voice, taut with growing excitement, exclaimed, "I can see the *Queen*, Dan!"

Scoville stilled his oars, twisted, and looked over his shoulder. The store boat loomed dimly, just a shapeless bulk at this distance, a dark outline against a slightly less darkened sky. Scoville began swinging the oars again, with slow and extreme care. The skiff stole along, clinging to the levee's shadow, and in time the stern of the store boat lifted above them, battered paddle wheel still. Scoville edged the skiff past this and along the outboard side of the boat.

Now they could see a faint fan of yellow light, spearing outward from a window of the storeroom of the *Island Queen*. But close in against the *Queen*'s weathered strakes the shadow was deep and sheltering, and Scoville, noiselessly shipping his oars, kept the skiff in this protective shadow, warding the skiff from contact with the larger hull, yet at the same time drawing it along with a hand on the store boat's fender.

There was no sign of sound or movement about the *Queen* anywhere, and, but for that single sliver of light farther forward, a man might have guessed the craft empty and deserted.

Foot by cautious foot, Scoville worked the skiff along toward the waist of the larger craft. And when he reached this spot, his warding hand was suddenly in slime, and a nauseous and unmistakable stench lay foul across the night's blackness. Tod Neely's murmur was just the faintest breath of sound.

"What is it, Dan? Smells kinda like old man Higbee's slaughter house, back at town."

"Exactly!" came back Scoville's whispered answer. "And it could explain a lot of things."

He stood up in the skiff, holding to the fender of the *Island Queen* with one hand, while with the other he felt of the cargo door above. It was a sliding door and either now locked shut, or too heavy to be moved without more purchase than Scoville had at the moment. But he wanted mightily to find out what lay beyond that door and he was trying to figure how he might manage this when Tod's murmur came again, breathless with urgency.

"Look out, Dan! Boat coming!"

Scoville froze, swung his head, and searched the deceiving night. Out there on the slough, still invisible, the approaching boat was still only a sound, the muffled, measured creak of swinging oars. Scoville stared until his eyes ached, but still saw nothing. Then, above the beat of the oars he heard the murmur of voices, and abruptly a low hail cut across the night.

"Branner—oh, Branner!"

Almost immediately there came answer in Pitch Branner's heavy voice from the low forward deck of the *Queen.*

"That you, Dickson?"

"Yeah. And I got Requa and Delbert with me."

"Good! Come on in."

The beat of the oars quickened, and then, caught for just a brief moment in the outermost reach of that spear of light, a skiff slid in and brought up with a soft bump against the side of the store boat. Scoville found himself holding his breath. That other skiff wasn't over thirty feet from where he and Tod crouched!

Men grunted as they climbed over the fender and to the foredeck of the *Queen*. Then there were some fading words by Pitch Branner as he and the new arrivals went into the *Queen*'s storeroom, words which Scoville could not clearly catch.

Scoville let out his breath in a long, soft sigh of relief. He knew a brief moment of hesitation. There would, he knew, be some very important talk go on in the storeroom of the *Queen*, talk he would have liked mightily to listen in on. But a try at eavesdropping would entail a strong risk of being discovered, and if that happened it could mean the upsetting of a plan which had at first been little more than the most nebulous of hunches, but which, over the hours and days, had become almost solid conviction. Discovery could also mean rough action, even gunfire, and with Tod Neely along, he could not afford to risk that. So now he pushed the skiff away from the side of the *Queen* and let it drift.

The tide had turned, was beginning to ebb. Scoville let it have its way with the skiff, and the drag of it carried the skiff slowly back along the way they had come, out past the stern of the store boat, past the loom of the paddle wheel, and on down into the open, still reaches of the slough.

He let the skiff drift silently for a good two hundred yards below the *Queen* before going cautiously to work with the oars again. And when he was sure they were well beyond all reasonable earshot, he spoke with a small note of exultation in his voice.

"Given time, Tod—a man generally ends up by locating a streak of luck."

"You mean, Dan—we were lucky we weren't seen by Maze Dickson and those others?" the boy asked.

"A little bit there, but mainly I was thinking from another angle. It's like this, Tod. Say there's a question hanging in front of you. At first you can't find any answer to that question at all. But you keep turning that question over and over in your head. You listen to what all men say and you watch what they do and you keep asking yourself why—why? Then, if you listen enough and watch enough and measure all men by their actions and their words, and keep on asking yourself why—why, you begin to maybe pick up a few parts of the answer to that big question. But no answer is enough unless you have all of it. Maybe for a time you figure that you're stumped, that you can't get all the answer. Then the streak of luck shows up. You bump into an angle just by chance, and that angle makes the answer complete. Tonight, we had our streak of luck."

Tod was frankly bewildered. This sort of talk was completely over his youthful head.

"I guess so, Dan," he mumbled. "I guess so."

Scoville laughed softly, but there was grimness in this as well as exultation. He quoted some words Tod had given to him earlier this day. " 'Too damn dumb to know his own hand in front of his face.' Tod, it always helps to have the other fellow underestimate you. Now we'll see just how fast this skiff of yours can go. For there are things I still got to do tonight."

It was close to midnight. Dan Scoville sat on a piling end at the Delta wharf, waiting and watching the upslough blackness. The town of Delta itself had turned in for the night; there was no glimmer of light anywhere, for even the Wagon Wheel was closed up. Scoville would have liked the comfort of his pipe, but he knew how the bite of tobacco smoke could carry on night's heavy air.

On arriving back at town from their boat trip, Scoville had directed Tod to turn in, and then had gone down to Ed Jethro's livery barn and had a short talk with the little stable owner. After which Jethro had saddled a horse and slipped out of town.

Returning to the office, Scoville had sat and smoked in the front room until satisfied that Tod was sound asleep in back. Then he had turned out the light, let himself out into the street, and made a cautious way up to this spot on the wharf. And here he had remained since, silent with his thoughts, watchful of the upslough approach. He was beginning to think he'd made a wrong guess in this matter, when he picked up the first faint beat of oars. He listened for a moment, then stole off the wharf and stood waiting just off the crest of the levee.

He heard the small boat come in to Maze Dickson's shanty boat, heard the murmur of voices and then the steps of someone climbing over the levee. Scoville dropped down on the town side of the levee and waited at the corner of a building where the levee road turned into town. The sound of steps came down the same way, and Scoville, flattened against the building, waited until the approaching figure was just even with him. Then, in two long strides he was out there and gripping that figure by the arm.

"Evening, Delbert," he said crisply. "Just the man I want to see."

George Delbert let out a grunt of surprise, then cursed softly and tried to jerk away.

Instantly Dan Scoville's grip turned steely and a tough, savage note bristled in his voice. "Don't try it, Delbert—or I'll bend a gun barrel over your head. You're coming along with me, and you're going to do some talking. You like to talk. Now you'll have your chance. Don't try and pull loose and don't try and yell. If you do, you get what I promised. Come along!"

By this time the lawyer recognized who it was had hold of him. He began to bluster.

"This is damned highhanded business, Scoville!

You can't push me around like this. I got my rights. I don't know what's biting you, but—"

"You'll find out," cut in Scoville. "Don't worry about your rights. That's one of the things we're going to talk about—rights. Also, wrongs. Come on!"

There was nothing else for Delbert to do but obey. He didn't struggle against Scoville's grip any more, and it seemed to Dan Scoville that he could, through this physical contact, sense an uneasy trembling in this man.

They went along the street to Ed Jethro's livery barn, turned in through the blackness of it, and located the door to the harness room. Still holding his man, Scoville found a match with his free hand, snapped it alight, and, as the faint glow shoved back some of the small room's darkness, pushed George Delbert into a chair. Then, before the match could go out, Scoville lifted the chimney from the lamp and touched the match to the wick. The lamp caught, and Scoville pushed the chimney back into place and turned up the flame.

"Now," he said, "just in case—we'll have a look. Stand up!"

Delbert obeyed, and Scoville frisked him swiftly, coming up with a small derringer from an inner pocket. Scoville stared bleakly at Delbert as he tossed the snub-nosed weapon up and down in his hand.

"Not so good, Delbert—not so good. A lawyer isn't supposed to pack a gun. His knowledge of the law is all the weapon he needs. Or that is the general supposition."

Delbert licked his lips, his froggy eyes showing a hard shine in the lamplight. "My knowledge of the law tells me that you've no legal right to treat me this way and that—"

Scoville waved a weary hand. "Save it, Delbert—save it. You'll have your chance later. Now we got a little waiting to do. You might as well relax."

Scoville got out his pipe, took another chair, and slouched deep in it. Here in this room it was still faintly warm from the stored-up warmth of the day now hours past. The little room was full of the not unpleasant, earthy odor of horses and their gear; of leather and harness soap and of sun-cured hay. And of the ammoniac reminder of the stable itself.

Night's stillness was complete, except for a minutia of sound which could hardly be rated as sound at all. Like the faint rustlings and squeakings and soft scurryings of mice in the hayloft overhead. And because of that stillness, Scoville caught the faint thump of hoofs out in front of the stable and then the low murmur of voices. He stood up quickly and moved to the door of the harness room and sent out a quiet call.

"Ed?"

"Yeah, Dan. Got your man here and—"

"Good!" cut in Scoville. "Leave him there. You come here."

Little Ed Jethro was just soft sound rustling through the dark until he stepped into the room. He stared in surprise at sight of George Delbert. Scoville handed the stable owner his gun.

"You'll get it all pretty quick, Ed. In the meantime—keep an eye on Delbert. Hardly think he'll try anything, but he might. I'll be right back."

Before Jethro could argue, Scoville stepped past him and moved through the dark of the main stable. Again he called softly.

"Logan?"

Cole Logan's heavy growl came back to him. "Yeah. What the hell's this all about? If you wanted to see me, why didn't you ride out to the ranch instead of sending Jethro after me?"

"Had another chore to do. I don't think you'll begrudge the ride after you've heard what I have to say. Rest yourself."

Scoville hunkered down on his heels, his shoulders against an inner wall of the stable. Logan found place beside him, grumbling. "Black as the inside of a cat in here. Now—I'm listening."

"I'll start," murmured Scoville, "by telling you something that Sheriff Frank Ide once said to me. It ran about like this. The answer to a human problem is not always the apparently obvious one. For most men act to further their own ends and they talk to the same purpose. So a smart law man listens and watches and questions motives and then balances his judgment against what he sees and hears. And if he does that shrewdly enough, then the chances are he'll eventually come up with the right answer."

"Makes sense," growled Logan. "But what's that got to do with me?"

"It's like this," Scoville said. "I'm laying my cards wide open on the table, and I want you to do the same, understanding that there's nothing personal about it. When I first hit Delta, I ran into a mixture of opinion concerning you. Some of it came from events I saw with my own eyes and from the personal clashes I had with you. Some I got from others. There were places where I heard you damned outright, without modification. In others I heard some criticism of you, but it was softened by the admission that in all the fundamentals you were a sound man."

Cole Logan gave a low, grim laugh. "Interesting. Go on."

"The people who gave off that last opinion were the kind I'd call fair people, whose opinions a man could safely believe in. They felt that you were mistaken in your idea that you had the right to set yourself up as the law on Middle Island, but at the same time they gave you credit for being quite sincere in that mistaken purpose, and that you were not doing it from purely selfish motives. Beyond that difference, they respected and admired you."

"Good to know I got some friends," rumbled Logan. "I've wondered about that at times."

"Then," resumed Scoville, "there was the other side, those who damned you outright, and there were angles there that didn't satisfy me, so I reserved judgment. For I was remembering what Frank Ide had told me and I wondered if maybe these people, or at least some of them, weren't against you for some selfish reason of their own, without regard for the actual facts. So I kept my own counsel and tried to figure out motives. From it all, a picture began to form. It could still be the wrong one. I'll know for sure, one way or the other, before too long. Mind answering a few questions?"

Cole Logan was listening intently, intrigued and deeply interested. He stirred slightly. "Hell, no! Let's have them."

"What," asked Scoville slowly, "started the first trouble between you and Ward Requa? Maybe not exactly trouble, but at least animosity?"

Cole Logan was silent for a moment, then spoke gravely.

"Mainly, I guess, that Requa and me just never did, or could, get along. Happens that way sometimes, you know. Two men meet, have a good look at each other, and from then on hate each other's guts forever." Logan hesitated a little before going on. "Then there was Nora Baine. She's a grand girl, but she never had any use for Requa, either. Always said the man was sly and tricky. Anyway, Requa insisted on paying his attentions to her, even though she showed him plainly that she wanted no truck with him at all. Oh, all very polite and proper, you understand, was his attitude, though he knew it was pure annoyance to Nora. To this day he never misses a chance to force Nora to recognize him, liking to pick his time and spot when others are around, so Nora can't ignore him as she'd like to, without making the situation marked and awkward. And all the time there's that damned sneering, sarcastic look in back of his pose of being a gentleman."

"Know what you mean," nodded Scoville. "Saw something of that in Bill Profitt's store the first day I hit Delta."

"Well," went on Logan, "it was this and that, small things building up to big ones. You know how that can come about. Anyway, one day Requa and I tangled. I guess I gave him a pretty stiff going over. Nora—" and here a faint thread of grim humor crept into Logan's voice, "Nora gave me ruddy hell for that. Since then, Requa and I have walked stiff-legged around each other, but there's been no more open clashes."

"What do you know about George Delbert?" asked Scoville.

Logan gave a grunt of contempt. "That loud-mouthed hypocrite! Always reminds me of a damn poodle dog, full of yap and noise and nothing else. I never figured him worth paying any attention to."

"I understand," probed Scoville, "that somebody took a shot at Delbert. When he was in Delta the first time and had that office I got now. The bullet hole in the wall was pointed out to me."

"I know," growled Logan. "The talk's been that I or one of the Logan outfit threw that shot. Damn lie, of course. If I felt Delbert was getting in my way, I might give him a boot in the pants, but I'd sure never waste a bullet on him. Oh, I've been damned for that and for a lot of other things I had nothing to do with. Like the story that I was responsible for making an orphan of that kid, Tod Neely. Another lie. The kid's father was just another shanty-boater who was never backward about eating Logan beef any time he got the chance. I warned him about it a couple of times, saying I'd run him off Middle Island if he didn't quit it, same as I warned Bid Hazen. But I had no more to do with his death than I did that of Hazen."

"I'm sure of that," murmured Scoville. "If I wasn't, you wouldn't be here tonight, healthy and able."

Cole Logan stirred again. "You're referring, of

course, to that little affair the day I met up with you and Loren, riding away from Mal Baine's place," he said gruffly. "Been thinking a lot about that. Biggest damn-fool play I ever made in my life, and I've made my share, I guess. I must have been loco. Anyhow, the way it came out it sure jarred things loose in this thick skull of mine. I might as well admit I've got things figured out pretty clear at last. If I didn't have, I wouldn't have ridden in here tonight. So I'll say right now that there'll be no more quarrel between you and me, Scoville, as to who runs the law on Middle Island. Your kind was bound to come. You're here, and what you say goes!"

"This," exclaimed Scoville fervently, "is what I've been wishing for. Now we can work together. We'll go into the harness room and you just listen. I'll do the talking."

Scoville straightened to his feet, paused for a last question. "Find any trace of Rack, yet?"

"No," rumbled Logan, a harshness coming over him. "That's one thing I want understood. Rack's my responsibility. I let him grow into what he is. My chore to take care of him."

To this Dan Scoville made mental reservation, but said nothing aloud.

XI—Night Parley

When they stepped into the harness room, Dan Scoville was watching George Delbert intently. When the lawyer's protuberant eyes moved past him to the big-shouldered, dark-faced figure of Cole Logan, Scoville saw Delbert start visibly and run the tip of his tongue across his lips. Logan showed his own small surprise at sight of Delbert, then stepped over and sat on the edge of the bunk. Ed Jethro looked inquiringly at Scoville, who nodded, accepted his gun from Jethro, and dropped it into the holster.

Scoville squared himself in front of Delbert and said, "Make yourselves comfortable, gentlemen. This could take a little time. All depending, of course, on how much co-operation Mister Delbert decides to show."

George Delbert licked his lips again. "I got my rights. I—"

"Just now you haven't a right in the world," interrupted Scoville calmly. "For there come times when, to get at the truth, it becomes necessary to take off the gloves. They're off, now!"

He repacked his pipe, lit it, and drew in a lungful of smoke.

"The main reason I'm here, Delbert, is because

you showed up in Riverton, setting up a great hue and cry about injustices being done on Middle Island by one Cole Logan, under the mask of enforcing some kind of law. You yelped to Sheriff Frank Ide, who didn't take too much stock in you. So then you ran to the county commissioners, who got on Frank Ide's neck about it. So he sent me down here to see what it was all about. Now that we got that part of the picture clear, we'll go on with the rest of it."

Scoville's glance bored coldly at the lawyer. "Delbert, there are some men who act through honest conviction, and who put that conviction above everything else. But they are few, and I can't see you as one of them. So, the only other answer is that you've got a selfish stake in this thing somewhere, a goal of personal gain. It certainly isn't through the channel of legitimate fees for legal work performed. I just can't see where there is even a starvation living for an honest lawyer in Delta. For instance, how many legal fees did you ever earn from Cole Logan or Mal Baine?"

"I can answer that," put in Cole Logan. "None!"

Scoville nodded. "And certainly I've seen no shanty-boater with enough money to make your efforts in his behalf profitable. So. I've got to come to the conviction that your real purpose in being here on Middle Island is other than you've advertised."

He paused to run a freshening match across the bowl of his pipe. "Now we'll get at another angle. When I arrived here, I heard all manner of talk from certain people against Cole Logan. I also heard talk in his favor. And those who talked in his favor were the kind of people it was easier to believe than the other sort, of whom you were one. So an idea began to grow in my mind. Like this.

"Cole Logan was too tough a handful to get rid of by those who were against him, without somebody's hand being shown too plainly. A much safer plan was to get somebody like me in here, and, through talk and other more rotten and cruel means, set me against Logan in a show-down which Logan was bound to lose, because the weight of constituted law was all behind me and against him. And then, with Cole Logan, the strong man on Middle Island, out of the way, the schemers could get on with their ambitions. Am I shooting close, Delbert?"

The lawyer tried to put sarcasm into his blurted answer. "Of all the wild talk I ever heard, that's the worst and craziest, Scoville." But in the thin yellow glow of the lamp, Dan Scoville could see a trickle of sweat run down Delbert's face.

"I don't think so," Scoville rapped. "I think I'm not only shooting close, but that I'm hitting dead center. Now a little question. Just what was the purpose of that meeting you and Ward Requa and

Maze Dickson had with Pitch Branner tonight on Branner's store boat?"

George Delbert hadn't been expecting anything like this. It came at him with the impact of a sudden blow, and he jerked forward in his chair, then swallowed thickly before he could manage an answer. "I—I don't know what you're talking about."

Scoville stepped closer and his voice ran harsh. "You know damned well what I'm talking about. You and Requa and Dickson visited with Branner on the *Island Queen*, where she's tied up at Pike's Landing. I know, because I saw you. So quit the lying and tell me what it was all about?"

Delbert slouched in his chair, turned sullen and silent. Scoville stared bleakly at him for a moment, then began taking short turns up and down the little room, speaking to no one in particular, like a man arranging his thoughts out loud.

"It will make a pretty vicious line of evidence for a jury up in the courtroom at Riverton to listen to. A shanty-boater named Neely, found floating in Cross Over Slough, with a bullet through him and a length of rope still around his neck. Couldn't hardly blame that on some shanty-boat feud, for if one shanty-boater wanted to get rid of another of his kind, he wouldn't go to the trouble of hanging him. He'd slip a knife into him, or knock his head in with an oar butt, or something like that. I wonder who it was found Jack Neely's body?"

"That," said Ed Jethro, "I can answer, Dan. Maze Dickson did. Said he'd run across Neely's body while he was out fishing."

Scoville swung his head. "Thanks, Ed—thanks. That's another link that fits the chain perfectly. And certain people immediately started talk that Cole Logan was responsible for Neely's death. All of which helped in getting Frank Ide to send a deputy to Delta. So I was sent here. And then, after a little interval of time, when Logan and I had not cut each other's throats, a new incentive was added. Bid Hazen was lynched. Now that, the schemers figured, would certainly send me storming after Cole Logan's scalp. For the same people who had talked against Logan before immediately started more talk that Logan was certainly the one responsible for Hazen's death."

Scoville swung around, facing George Delbert directly again, a lean, accusing finger stabbing under the lawyer's nose. "You in particular didn't lose any time, Delbert. You braced me in my office with a bunch of shanty-boaters behind you and when you didn't get anywhere, you marched up and down town, bellowing about the rights of men, threatening to organize the shanty-boaters and take matters into your own hands. Delbert, you were a little too eager. So now I'm asking you a question and I want a straight answer. Where were you the night Bid Hazen was lynched?"

Again there was sweat running down the lawyer's puffy, florid cheeks, while his bulging eyes took on a fixed, almost glassy stare. "I wasn't there!" he gulped. "I had nothing to do with—"

"Who was there? Ward Requa, maybe? And his two riders? Jake is the name of one of them, I believe."

"Jake Andrus," put in Ed Jethro, in little more than a breathless whisper.

"Thanks, Ed," said Scoville again. "You see, Delbert, I know that this Jake Andrus was riding that night—that foggy night which was a good one for murder. So Mister Andrus will have his chance to talk. He'll probably be only too glad to turn state's evidence. And, as a lawyer, Delbert, you know the advantage of turning state's evidence. It generally gets a lighter sentence for the person who talks. Well, you've had your chance. Andrus will probably be a lot smarter than you. He'll welcome the chance to save his hide."

Scoville turned away. "Ed," he said to Jethro, "I'm going to leave Delbert in your care. We'll tie him down to your bunk. Then Cole and I are going out to collect this Jake Andrus. All right with you?"

"Sure," answered the little stablekeeper. "Sure, Dan. Glad to help any way I can." Then, with a rush of pure inspiration, "Man—you sure have collected a lot of evidence."

Scoville showed him a tight grin. "You've heard only a small part of it, Ed. I know a lot of things I'm not supposed to. I was played as being too dumb to know my own hand in front of my face. Understand that was a remark made by Mister Requa to friend Delbert, here. Well, it always pays to act stupid to those who think they're smart."

He turned to Delbert again. "All right, you. Over on that bunk. I'm going to make sure I keep you safe for delivery to Sheriff Frank Ide and to the District Attorney at Riverton. They'll hang your hide up to dry."

Now the sweat was really running down Delbert's face. The pressure of this thing had finally dug in to where it hurt. How much did this lean, cold-eyed deputy really know? He'd already shown that he knew far more than Delbert had dreamed. And Delbert did know all about state's evidence. It could win something for a man. George Delbert wished he could think more clearly. But just now his mind seemed numbed, because at heart the man was craven and now a great fear was rising in him.

He jerked spasmodically, as Scoville's grip settled on his shoulder and Scoville's voice lashed him. "Come on—over on that bunk! I've wasted too much time with you already."

The dam broke. "Wait!" gulped Delbert. "Wait! I—I'll talk—I'll talk—!"

He didn't see the glint of relief that flashed in Dan Scoville's eyes as Scoville dropped his hand and stepped back. For that fear that was in him was pushing behind his eyes and blinding him to such minor things.

When George Delbert started to talk, his words at first came slow and halting, but swiftly his tone pitched higher and his words faster.

"It's all Ward Requa's fault. The idea was all his from the start. It came from two things—his hate of Cole Logan and his jealousy over Logan's size on this island. Then there was the fact that the Baine girl plainly preferred Logan to him. So Requa was out to break Logan and get rid of him. Requa started out by encouraging some of the shanty-boaters to slow-elk Block L cattle. When they picked up some of Mal Baine's stock, that didn't worry Requa either, for in the long run he intended getting rid of Baine, too—when all of Middle Island would have been open for him to take over."

"A few slow-elked cattle wouldn't break either Cole Logan or Mal Baine," put in Scoville. "Things go deeper than that."

"I know they do—I know they do. Give me a chance." Now that he had started, Delbert seemed almost feverishly anxious to get it all off his chest. "Slow-elked cattle were only a start.

Bait that was. To get Logan and Baine—Logan in particular—to playing rough, the rougher the better. Which would bring Frank Ide's office down around Logan's ears. The shanty-boaters didn't realize how Requa was using them—only Maze Dickson was really in on the scheme."

"And Pitch Branner—with his store boat?" put in Scoville.

"Yeah. Branner, too. One of them did begin to wise up, and he tackled Requa about it. That was Jack Neely."

"Ah!" murmured Scoville. "Go on."

"Requa figured to kill two birds with one stone with Neely. Shut him up and throw more blame Logan's way. It was common knowledge that Logan had given Neely hell and threatened to run him off the island. So Requa took care of Neely and arranged for Dickson to find the body and start the talk of Logan being responsible."

A deep growl began to rumble in Cole Logan's throat, but Scoville quieted him with a warning headshake. Scoville kept the pressure on Delbert.

"And, of course, the Bid Hazen affair was more of the same?"

"That's right." Delbert was holding nothing back; he was all quaking jelly. "The first day in town when you and Logan braced each other, Requa was in Profitt's store. He heard Logan make the threat to you that he'd hang Hazen, first time he got the chance. So, when you didn't seem to be going after Logan too hard, he figured another chunk of bait would sure make you take action. Then—he strung Hazen."

"Nice fellow—Requa!" gritted Scoville. "How about your part in the mess? How did you get tied in?"

Delbert hesitated a moment, then spoke thickly. "I was broke. I'd made a mistake in trying to set up a law practice here in Delta. There just wasn't any. Requa was smart enough to see that I was hard up—desperate for money. So he made me a proposition. In spite of what he'd already done, it hadn't been enough to stir up any action from Frank Ide's office. He needed somebody to go outside and raise a stink about things. He offered me a thousand dollars to go to Riverton and raise a ruckus that would force Ide to send in a deputy who would tangle with Cole Logan and get Logan out of the way."

"Smooth hombre," said Scoville. "If he'd gone to Riverton himself it would have shown his hand. So he bought you. You hold the price of your soul pretty cheap, don't you, Delbert?"

The lawyer shrugged. "When you're broke, a thousand dollars can look like a fortune. Besides, I was to get more after Logan had been smashed and Requa was able to take over on the island."

Scoville studied Delbert, a deep contempt in his eyes. "There's a bullet hole in the wall over at the office. It was supposed to have been a slug turned your way by Logan or one of his outfit. More window dressing?"

Delbert nodded. "An excuse for me to pull freight as abruptly as I did. Another idea of Requa's."

"That fellow was just full of ideas, wasn't he?" Scoville took a turn up and down the room, swung to face Delbert once more. "Now about that little meeting that took place on the *Island Queen* tonight. You've probably been wondering how I knew about it. Well, I wanted a little closer look at something about the boat than I'd been able to get when she was tied up here at town—in a way that wouldn't warn Branner. So I was alongside the *Queen* tonight in a skiff. When you and Requa and Maze Dickson went aboard, I wasn't fifty feet away from you.

"Branner is pretty careless about his boat, isn't he? Should keep it cleaner. Shouldn't let the drain from a meat room dribble down the side of the boat where it could attract flies and leave stains. When I saw that it made me wonder about these slow-elking stories. Now a shanty-boater or two might be able to slow-elk one critter and get away with the meat in a skiff. But there have been times when six or eight or ten critters have disappeared at an instance. That meant bigger operations than just those of a casual shanty-boater. How right am I?"

"You've hit it," admitted Delbert. "Branner's been hauling slow-elked beef and selling it cheap all up and down the sloughs and among the islands. He can afford to sell it cheap, for it costs him damn little to get it. He aims to take on another load tomorrow. Rack Logan's going to help him—"

"What!" In one leap Cole Logan was facing Delbert, towering over him, his voice a furious rumble. "What kind of a lie is that? What do you know about Rack? Where is he—?"

Delbert cringed, his froggy eyes staring up at the big dark man. A cornered shrillness edged his words.

"Rack's at the Arrowhead—with Requa. He told Requa he was through with the Logan family—that you'd sided with Scoville against him. So he's out to get even. Said he wanted to see you busted and that he was going to work on Logan cattle until there wasn't a Block L critter left. That's about Rack."

Cole Logan's big hands worked and flexed, half reached for Delbert's throat. "Why you slimy, lying—!"

Dan Scoville put a hand on Cole's shoulder, pulled him back. "Easy, Cole," he cautioned. "Let me handle this. We're getting what we've been after—answers."

For a moment Cole fought against the pull of Scoville's grip, then gave way, growling deep in his throat. Scoville took his place in front of the lawyer.

"You said Branner aimed to pick up another load of beef tomorrow, Delbert. Where?"

"Off—off the mouth of Mudbank. He's going to tie the *Island Queen* up there. And from some place close by Mudbank is where they aim to pick up the beef. Now—now what about me? What break do I get?"

"Better than you deserve, probably," answered Scoville curtly. "You've talked, and the Court will remember that. But for the present you're going to stay right in this room, tied to that bunk. And Ed Jethro is going to keep an eye on you, with my permission to kill you if you make any fuss. Cole, you and I have things to do. You, of course, know where this Mudbank is?"

"I know," rumbled Cole.

"Good! We'll be there."

XII—Swamp Battle

They lounged in reasonable comfort on a thick pad of tramped-down tules and cattails, which was enough to hold them off the wet and oozy swamp earth beneath. But it was not enough to shut off the dank and noisome breath which this swamp earth sent up, and it grew in its offensiveness as the sun climbed higher and sent its heat beating down upon them. A little in back and to one side, their horses stood ground-reined in the middle of a particularly lofty-growing clump of tules, and they could hear the soggy lift and thump of hoofs as the horses stamped restlessly against the torment of mosquitoes and swamp flies.

Mudbank, so Cole Logan had explained to Dan Scoville, was a sort of blind lagoon which broke off from the main slough to the east of Middle Island and which wound back into the island for a considerable distance before ending up in an extensive swamp area. Cattle persisted in hanging out along the edges of this swamp area, and it would be, Cole declared, a fairly safe place for slow-elkers to work in, for the high-growing tules would hide the thieves at their work.

Beyond this explanation, Cole had had little to say as he and Scoville rode out there in the first gray light of dawn, selected this hiding place where they now lay, and settled themselves for a long wait. There was a dark brooding in Cole, a bleakness about his mouth and bitterness in his eyes.

Cole was thinking about Rack, and about what George Delbert had told about Rack. Back in Ed Jethro's harness room, Cole had branded Delbert's words about Rack as a lie, but in his heart he knew that Delbert had been speaking the truth. Because it was something that Delbert would never have thought to make up or, in his craven condition, tried to put over. No, Delbert had given them the truth about Rack, and this truth ground at Cole's very soul.

For it was the final straw to shatter the great fabric of pride which Cole had built up around the Logans. Deep down, Cole had always known that Rack was poor stuff, that there was a mean and vengeful streak in him, but he had never dreamed that Rack could slide so far down as to side with the enemy against his own blood in this manner and to turn cattle thief to do it. Right now, Cole Logan was feeding on gall and wormwood.

Dan Scoville knew full well what was in Cole's mind and he made no mention of Rack, instead keeping his comments faintly humorous as he slapped at the mosquitoes and swore at the thick offensiveness of the swamp's breath and the increasing heat of the sun as it climbed even higher. He got little response here from Cole, however, and so they fell into silence, each man sunk in his own thoughts.

They built smokes and waited stoically while the slow hours moved by. The sun arched to the zenith and the heat of it piled up, intensified by the humidity which steamed up from the swampy earth beneath them. Over at the edge of the swamp a cow bawled forlornly, and the sound brought Cole Logan to his feet for a long look around. When he hunkered down again he spoke with harsh abruptness.

"I'm saying something I said before, Scoville. Rack's my responsibility. I'll take care of him."

Scoville half nodded, making a silent reservation of his own concerning this question.

Now that he had broken through his brooding thoughts, Cole went on.

"I've long known Rack wasn't like the rest of us. I guess the Logan family isn't the first to spawn a maverick, a throwback, but this move of Rack's sure hits where it hurts. I'd have thought more of him if he'd have stood his ground and shot my head off. But to side in with Requa and set out to cut the substance away from his own family—that makes him mighty low. So—he belongs to me!"

"We'll wait," said Scoville quietly. "Maybe it won't come to that." Then Scoville laughed softly. "Know what I've been thinking about,

Cole? Well, about how, not so long ago, you and me beat hell out of each other. Now, here we are together, working in common cause."

Cole's dark mood lightened somewhat. He even showed a small grin. "Beat hell out of each other is right. That was a brawl! Never got hit so hard in my life. When you put me down with that first punch, I just couldn't believe it had happened. First time I'd ever been knocked off my feet. But there I was, flat on my back in the dust." His glance met Scoville's in sudden gravity. "I'd have thought you'd have hated me forever for that day. Another time I was a damned fool!"

Scoville smiled. "Not at all. A good licking now and then keeps a man's ego cut down to size. Well, I sure took one. And it was worth it, all things considered. So—forget it. I have."

"You," said Cole quietly, "are a damned generous man, Dan Scoville."

It began to look like they were going to draw a blank. From time to time, one or the other of them would stand and make a cautious and careful survey over the tule tops, but they saw nothing of the *Island Queen*, or any movement at all, for that matter. But there was life in this swamp. From time to time, they heard the sucking plod of cattle hoofs passing at not too great a distance, heard the rustle of tules as heavy, bovine bodies pushed through. Once a burly two-year-old steer came squarely upon them, stared for a moment in startled wonder, then snorted and went lunging off.

"Wonder if that damned shyster of a Delbert was lying to us?" growled Cole, after another long wait. "Look where that sun is. We've had damn near a day of it, lying out here. Won't be too long before sundown again."

Dan Scoville shook his head. "I don't think Delbert was lying. He knew that the minute he first made admission of any sort, he might as well give us the whole story. I think he did. And, man! you got no idea how glad I was when he did. Because I was running a pretty long bluff there. Oh, I had things figured out in my own mind, and was reasonably sure I was hitting pretty close to the truth. But if Delbert hadn't opened up, I could have been hard put to prove a lot of things. But now, with him as a witness, I can clean up the whole affair."

"What made you think he'd talk?" Cole asked.

"I've been packing this star quite a while," said Scoville, building up another smoke. "Like in any other trade, you learn some of the tricks. And you get the knack of judging people. A fellow like Delbert, full of bluster and talk, is nearly always a weak reed. You take them by surprise, you throw a scare into them, make them believe you know more than you really do, and they generally start coming apart. Show me a small-time crook and I'm looking at a man who puts the safety of his own hide above everything else, once the chips are down. I figured Delbert that way—and it worked."

"You're going after Ward Requa for murder?"

Scoville's jaw stole out. "For murder—no less. But I'm playing the game this way because I want Branner, too. If I went straight after Requa, then Branner would scare off and I'd have nothing on him I could really cinch him with. But if I can catch him in the act—!"

Scoville stretched restlessly, stood up for another look around. He stiffened, then said quietly, "Delbert didn't lie, Cole. Yonder's the *Island Queen*!"

Cole lunged to his feet, stared as Scoville pointed. Beyond the screen of trees along the distant levee top, the top hamper of the *Queen* was a slow-moving bulk, heading south along Ten Mile Slough. They watched that slow progress come to a complete halt, just north of when Mudbank broke away from Ten Mile. And that was all they saw for another interval of time, during which the sun sank and finally set. Then there came movement on the levee top. Men, coming down across the levee and down into the swamp. And two other men, mounted, riding along the levee from the north. These also left the levee and moved into the edge of the swamp.

"That's it!" growled Cole. "And they sure picked the right time of day. Late enough for the ranch hands to all have headed in to headquarters for supper, but early enough to have daylight left to work in. That Branner is a slick one. Either that, or I've been awful thick-headed not to have figured him and the *Island Queen* in on this slow-elking business. For many's the head of cattle I've shipped off this island by barge. That's how Mal Baine and me, and Ward Requa, too, for that matter, have always marketed our cattle. Jim Herrin comes up from San Francisco with his tug and barge and hauls them out for us. This should have suggested to me that Branner and his boat would have a hand in the slow-elking, but for some reason that never entered my mind. I've always looked on the *Island Queen* as just what she's supposed to be, a battered old scow of a store boat, prowling the sloughs, selling odd junk to the shanty-boaters."

They waited and watched a little longer, and then Cole said, "They won't come in this far, Dan. We'll have to go to meet them."

"This will cost you a few head of stock, Cole," reminded Scoville. "For I want to catch them redhanded with the evidence. That's the way the law must work. When I make this arrest, I want it to stick."

"That's all right," growled Cole. "Just so we put a quietus on this sort of business, once and for all. Let's go!"

They went afoot, leading their horses. To have

climbed into their saddles would have lifted them above the tule tops where they were virtually certain to be seen. Even so, they had to move carefully, keeping always to the higher growth.

It was tough going. They fought through tangled masses of tules, yards across. Underfoot it was always treacherous, and in places they lunged and floundered through muck up to their knees, the horses making heavy work of it behind them.

Out ahead they heard the faint, keen crack of a gun. Cole cursed. "They're shooting the critters they want with a light rifle. Twenty-five twenty, or something like that."

Half a dozen times they heard that whipping report and the last time not too far ahead. They heard the plunging rush and snorting of startled, harried cattle scattering through the coverts. From the edge of a thick mass of towering tule growth, they glimpsed an area ahead which seemed comparatively open after what they had so far come through, a stretch of a good hundred yards where only a few thin clumps of tules lifted, the rest covered by a near waist-high tangle of pigweed and salt grass. This would offer little concealment to a man, none at all for a horse.

Dan Scoville scrubbed the sweat from his face with a wiping shirt sleeve. "Have to leave the horses here, Cole. And we'll need luck to get across this, even so, without being seen."

A critter broke from the far side of the clearing, charging at an angle toward them and on past at a lunging run, shaking its head wildly, hoofs churning up a splatter of odorous muck. Down one side of its neck ran a crimson stream and on its hip a Block L brand showed plainly. Cole swore again.

"They made a bad shot on that one. Maybe it'll live and maybe it won't. If the flies get into that open wound, it's gone. Come on!"

They went out into the open, half crouched. After the concealment of the taller growth behind, Dan Scoville had a queer feeling of nakedness out in this shorter stuff. He wondered if, out ahead where the tules lifted high and thick again, eyes were not watching him and Cole, if maybe gun muzzles were not already trained on them, waiting only for the distance to shorten enough to make a shot absolutely certain. A prickling ran up his spine and his glance searched the tangle ahead with desperate intentness.

Once his glance lifted and he was startled at how close the top hamper of the *Island Queen* loomed against the twilight sky. He and Cole Logan had come considerable distance since beginning their strange stalk.

Halfway across the opening, now. Three quarters of the way. Sweat streamed down Scoville's face, stung his eyes. The smell of the swamp was a turgid, invisible thing, yet it seemed to have a thick substance to it that choked the air from a man's lungs.

More tules at last, a thick barrier of them. Scoville let out a long, shuddering breath of relief as he and Cole pushed into this shelter, paused to listen and get their breath. Voices ahead, only a little way ahead, but an indistinguishable murmur. Scoville jerked his head and he and Cole went on, cautiously now, parting the tangle of tules with their hands before edging their bodies along, feeling out each step with slow care.

The tule mass they were working through now was not of too great extent, being more of a fringe between one comparative open and another much like it. Dan Scoville and Cole Logan were almost through before they realized this. They brought up short at sound of words again, these in the droning thinness of tone that was unmistakable. It was Rack Logan's voice they heard.

"All right, Requa—these two are ready. Let's get them out of here!"

A rising growl of fury rumbled in Cole Logan's throat. Dan Scoville made a grab for him, but Cole was just beyond reach. And Cole, driving ahead like a maddened bull, broke into the open. Dan Scoville had no recourse but to follow.

His whipping glance took in what lay before them. Not twenty yards away, two freshly eviscerated beef carcasses lay. Farther along were three others, a man working over each with a flashing knife. About the necks of the two nearer carcasses, riata loops were drawn tight, the ropes reaching up to the saddles of two edgy, nervous horses that were restless and full of alarm at the smell of blood and steaming entrails. In one of the saddles Ward Requa sat. And Rack Logan was just reaching for the stirrup of the other.

"Rack!" yelled Cole Logan. "You—Rack! What the hell is this?"

For a long, breathless second it was like a tableau, all things frozen into utter, poised lack of motion. Then Dan Scoville's order struck harshly across the clearing.

"Steady—everybody! This is an arrest. Steady—!"

They were words wasted on Rack Logan and Ward Requa. Rack, two-legged wolf that he was, moved with the speed of one. He flung away from his horse, grabbing for his gun. The glare of his baleful, hooded eyes was on Dan Scoville.

There was no way out of this thing—no half-way measure that was good enough; no way of stopping it short of gunwork and the somber ending that must follow. Dan Scoville had sensed this, even when he challenged. And for that reason he'd been reaching for his gun with the first word.

It was well that he did so, for it gave him the thin fraction of time which he needed against

Rack; Rack Logan was a striking reptile at this sort of grim business.

Scoville's gun thudded flatly, leaped in recoil. He saw Rack lurch, and Rack's shot, late by that split second, was a whisper of venom past Scoville's throat. Rack fell back against his horse, and when the spooked animal shied away, Rack fell full length into the pigweed and lay still.

Another gun bellowed, and Cole Logan cursed and went down on his hands and knees. Ward Requa, gun in one hand, was working frantically with the other to throw off the dally he'd taken about his saddle horn, a move to free himself and his horse from the rope that led down to one of those beef carcasses.

Scoville yelled at him, "Requa! Drop that gun! Drop it—!"

Instead, Requa slashed a shot. But Requa's horse was spooking, now, too, and the shot was low, short of Scoville, splattering ooze and swamp mud.

Scoville pushed his gun level, yelled again. "Last chance, Requa. Drop it!"

His final word was lost in the rumble of Cole Logan's gun as it smashed the echoes about. Cole was on his knees, supporting himself with his left hand, had his gun free in his right. He shot a second time.

Dan Scoville saw the bullet impact shake Ward Requa, saw Requa surge high in his saddle, his head back, as though he was trying to peer into some great distance. Then his head fell limply to one side and the rest of him followed it, and his fall was a heavy, sodden sound.

Scoville charged across the clearing toward the three men with the butcher knives, gun ready ahead of him.

"Don't you be fools enough to try it!"

They weren't. They were men frozen by the explosive surprise of this thing, by the fury of fleeting moments that had seen two men go down into huddled stillness, while a third, Cole Logan, was still floundering around, trying to regain his feet. They straightened slowly, knives falling from their hands, their arms lifting. One of them was Maze Dickson, the others the two deck hands from the *Island Queen.* Maze Dickson did glance at a light-calibered rifle lying close by, but that was the extent of his opposition.

Dan Scoville herded them back to where Cole Logan, half crouched now, was gripping with a hand at his left leg, halfway between knee and ankle. Cole's face was dark from a mixture of cooling fury and growing pain.

"You can't stand on a crippled leg," warned Scoville harshly. "Don't try!"

"It's not that bad," rumbled Cole in return. "The bone's still sound."

Cole's glance touched the crumpled figure of Rack, almost hidden in the pigweed. Then it came back to Scoville, whose harshness of tone turned to gruffness.

"I didn't want any shooting, Cole. But—"

"You had no choice," growled Cole. "Neither did I. Requa knocked this leg from under me on his first try and he was all set to go again. I missed him my first shot—but with the second—"

"Can you watch these three while I get our broncs?"

"Fly to it," nodded Cole.

Scoville went back and brought up their horses, swinging Cole's into place beside him.

"Got to get you into your saddle, Cole. I want a look at that leg of yours and I can't do it in this muck."

With Scoville's aiding shoulder, Cole managed it, a beading of cold sweat sliming his cheeks. Maze Dickson and the two deck hands of the *Island Queen*, stood sullen and subdued. There was no semblance of fight in any of them.

With his pocket knife, Scoville slit the leg of Cole's mud-smeared jeans, peeled the cloth back. There was more mud and there was seeping blood, and a blue-lipped hole where the bullet had gone in and a more ragged one where it had come out.

"Let's see you wiggle your foot," ordered Scoville.

Cole did so and Scoville sighed in relief. "The bone wasn't hit. That's the main thing."

He stripped off his neckerchief, bound it tightly about the leg, covering the wounds. “That’ll hold until you can get to town and have it fixed up right.”

“You want Pitch Branner, you better be going after him,” said Cole in his old, solid growl. “This ruckus may have spooked him and he’ll be pulling out in the *Island Queen*.”

“Minus two deck hands, I doubt he could manage it,” Scoville said. “Besides, if he heard the shots, he’ll probably figure it some more cow critters down.” He hesitated, then added in a low tone, “I’m sorry about Rack.”

Cole’s face settled into harsh, stern lines. “He turned renegade. He dragged the Logan name in the mud. He was out to rob his own kin. You gave him his chance and he wouldn’t take it. He asked for what he got. If you hadn’t cut down on him, I would have. It’s done. Put it out of your mind.”

Scoville turned to Maze Dickson and the two deck hands, his words crisp.

“Get Rack Logan and Ward Requa across their saddles and tie them there. Hurry up! Daylight’s running out on us.”

This was done. Then, at Scoville’s command, Dickson and the deck hands plodded toward the edge of the swamp, leading the two horses with their grisly burdens. Scoville and Cole Logan rode along behind. Scoville tried not to look at Rack’s limp figure. But Cole did, several times, and there was no relenting in the grim fixity of his glance.

Dan Scoville knew a sudden, deep weariness. The long wait out in the swamp with its sodden heat and foul breath, then the few savage moments when the guns blinked crimson and shouted hollow death across the world—these things took it out of a man.

His hunch had worked out, his judgment of men and their motives had been correct—judgment both of good men and bad. But he hadn't wanted this thing to end in a shootout. He'd wanted a clean arrest, and then the due processes of the written law to take care of the rest of it.

But Rack Logan and Ward Requa hadn't wanted it that way. Trapped, surprised, desperate—both of them, they had taken the long chance and failed.

They cleared the swamp area and moved across solid ground toward the levee and the slough beyond, where the *Island Queen* still lay motionless in the waters of Ten Mile. At the base of the levee, Scoville called a halt and dismounted.

"Keep an eye on these three, Cole."

Cole nodded, then cautioned, "Watch yourself, Dan. No telling what you'll find on board."

Scoville bent, took off his mud-caked spurs, straightened, wiped his hands on the legs of his jeans, drew his gun, and prowled up the levee slope through a dusk that was rapidly thickening toward darkness. On the levee top the *Island Queen* loomed before him. The cargo door at the waist of the craft was open, and a gangplank reached from this to the levee. Light was shining dimly beyond the cargo door.

Scoville stole carefully across the gangplank and through the cargo door. Here was a compartment about twelve feet square, with three transverse beams which held a row of meat hooks. A lantern, hanging from one of these hooks, threw its yellow glow about. Another door, opening in the inner wall of the compartment, was ajar about a foot and there was light beyond this, too. And a voice—Pitch Branner's voice.

"The boys must have put quite a few critters down, Hutch. Well, that's all right, too. We can handle them. And there's plenty of beef-hungry folks up and down the sloughs. We'll get rich yet, Hutch."

"No," said Dan Scoville, pushing open that inner door and stepping through, gun couched at his hip. "No, Branner—you'll never be rich. From now on you won't have to worry about money. The state will be feeding you for a long time. Now don't anybody get any foolish ideas!"

They were men stupefied, jaws dropped, eyes staring in disbelief. Two of them. Pitch Branner and a scrawny, rusty-haired character in greasy singlet and dungarees.

"You understand that you're under arrest, of course, both of you," rapped Scoville. "And the *Island Queen* will be heading back to Delta tonight. You won't be hauling any slow-elked beef, Branner. Instead, you'll have passengers—two of them dead. And some horses. All right—get outside on the levee, where I can keep an eye on you."

They offered no argument, set up no protest. They were not of the desperate, savage stuff that had been in Rack Logan and Ward Requa. These men were up to thievery, but nothing stronger. They slouched ahead of Scoville, out across the gangplank to the levee.

XIII—The Rendered Verdict

It was another dawn, growing swiftly, and with every passing moment its light brought more clearly into relief the details of the Arrowhead headquarters.

At a corner of the bunkhouse, Dan Scoville crouched, waiting. He was stiff with night's fading chill and grim with weariness, for it had been many, many hours since he had last slept. At the opposite corner of the bunkhouse, grizzled old Sage was also hunkered on his heels, and the door of the bunkhouse lay between him and Scoville. Across Sage's knees a sawed-off shotgun was balanced.

Sage's being here was his own idea, his own insistence, when he'd learned what Dan Scoville intended to do.

"You ain't," Sage had stated firmly, back in Delta, "goin' out alone to Requa's headquarters to collect Jake Andrus and Stony Crofts by yourself. Stony Crofts ain't so much, but Jake Andrus can be a pretty mean customer. Mebbe they'll be wonderin' where Ward Requa is, why he ain't come home. If they are, then they'll be on guard and plenty dangerous. If they ain't wonderin' about Requa, they may not be on guard, but Andrus can still be dangerous. So—

I'm goin' along, me and my old stage guard shotgun. That's final!"

In the face of this, Scoville had been unable to do anything but accept Sage's company, and he had to admit to a certain warm satisfaction over the old fellow's concern.

It had been midnight before they'd been able to get away from Delta. There had been many things to do. George Delbert had been taken from Ed Jethro's harness room, over onto the *Island Queen*, and Bill Profitt, once he'd listened to the whole grim and startling story, had been only too glad to lock up his store and help Jethro guard the prisoners, bunched on the *Island Queen.*

Cole Logan had been put to bed in Dan Scoville's bunk, and Molly Profitt brought in to doctor up Cole's leg wound. Cole had growled some objection to this, swearing he was able to ride on home, but Scoville had refused flatly even to listen to such an idea. After this, when Scoville stated his intention of heading for the Arrowhead to collect the two riders who had helped Ward Requa lynch Bid Hazen, was when Sage had stated his determination to go along.

Scoville and Sage had come up quietly to the Arrowhead layout, having left their horses well back and stealing in on foot. When they had heard the snores of the two sleeping men in the bunkhouse, Scoville's first idea was to go right on in. But when he realized that dawn was not too far away and that neither he nor Sage had any idea of the layout of the bunkhouse, he decided to play it a little safer.

There had been, he thought bleakly, enough shooting, enough dead men. And if he and Sage went blundering into this bunkhouse in the black dark, not sure of the location of bunks or table or chairs or any other furnishings, there was no surety of how the thing might turn out. It was, he decided, a time to use guile instead of direct force. So, he and Sage had taken position and settled down to wait matters out.

As the dawn light crept into the bunkhouse there came a stirring, the mutter of sleepy voices, the creak of bunk springs, and the thump of a boot heel on the floor. Dan Scoville looked over at Sage, nodded, and they both came to their feet.

Inside, a man coughed, cleared his throat harshly, then boot heels scuffed as the man came to the door, swung it open, and stepped out into the dawn light.

He was burly, dark-faced, and in need of a shave. He went completely still as Dan Scoville's voice reached him quietly.

"Just as you are, friend. Stay that way!"

The fellow stared, then his words came out in heavy, gravelly tones. And Scoville, remembering what Loren Logan had told him, knew that this was Jake Andrus.

"What the hell is this?" was Andrus' demand.

"An arrest," Scoville told him. "For participation in the murder of Bid Hazen. Come over this way!"

Jake Andrus looked at the gun in Scoville's hand. He was unarmed, himself, standing there just in his jeans and boots and shirt sleeves; bareheaded, his hair hanging ragged across his forehead and about his ears.

From the other side of Andrus, Sage reminded, "I'm here, too, Andrus. And packing buckshot. Better mind what Dan's tellin' you!"

The rider's lips thinned and his eyes burned. "Where's Requa?" he demanded in that hoarse, gravelly tone.

"Dead," said Scoville. "You heard me—come over here!"

Jake Andrus started to turn, as though to obey, but abruptly his thinned lips parted in a snarl of desperation and he dove for the doorway of the bunkhouse, trying to get inside.

He was halfway there when Dan Scoville's driving shoulder smashed into him and they both went down in a tangle, just inside the door. And Sage, driving past them, shotgun level at his hip, sent a yell ahead of him.

"Easy does it, Crofts! Or I'll buckshot you—I'll buckshot you—!"

There had been a Winchester rifle leaning against the bunkhouse wall just inside the door, and Jake Andrus had grabbed for this as he tried his desperate dive for sanctuary. Now, as he fought against the weight of Dan Scoville on his shoulders, he still tried to make some use of the rifle. But it was too big a weapon, too clumsy to get any use from in this kind of a tangle, and when Andrus, realizing this, tried to throw it aside and get a grip on Scoville, he left himself wide open to the short, slashing blow Scoville aimed with the weight of his belt gun. The heavy barrel of the Colt thudded home on Jake's head and the fellow grunted and went limp.

Scoville rolled clear and lunged to his feet, ready to back up Sage's hand. Sage didn't need it. He had the barrels of his shotgun jammed right against the chest of a lank, lantern-jawed figure who was still only half out of his blankets. Stony Crofts was well taken care of, wanted no part of useless resistance against this surprise attack.

"That was fast thinking and fast acting, Sage," said Scoville. "Your part, I mean. Thanks!"

Sage grinned crookedly. "Nothing like having an old hand around at times, Dan. Well, looks like we got what we came after."

It was a full two months later and Sage's stage was heading east again, and the world looked much the same here at Spanish Slough ferry as it had the first time Dan Scoville had seen it. Perhaps the dust was a little deeper along the levee road and the tules and sedge showing some change in color because of the advancing season. There was one real difference. Joe Imbaugh, the grizzled ferryman, had a new helper, a stocky redhead with a cheerful grin.

"What," asked Dan Scoville, as Sage carefully tooled the team and stage on to the ferry, "what became of Imbaugh's half-breed helper?"

Sage streaked the brown slough water with the darker stain of a mouthful of tobacco juice. "First day you showed here with that star of yours, the 'breed got the itchy foot, so Joe says. Apparently Spanish Slough wasn't far enough away from organized law. So the 'breed went lookin' for more distance."

With the ferry left behind and the stage kicking up its funnel of dust along the levee beside Cross Over Slough, Scoville mused over his change of feeling. The first time he'd seen this stretch of country he'd been anything but enthusiastic about it. Now it gave off a feeling of familiarity, and Scoville was all eagerness at returning.

He thought of the weeks that had passed since he had come out along this same road with Sage's stage bulging with prisoners. He'd known impatience over returning even then, but the law, as was its way, had been slow-moving and deliberate, and he'd had to remain in Riverton until every case was decided and settled. George Delbert, having turned state's evidence, had got off lightly, as had Maze Dickson and the deck hands of the *Island Queen.* They had been told to get out of the country and stay gone. Pitch Branner had taken a fairly heavy jail sentence, while Jake Andrus and Stony Crofts had missed the noose by a small margin, but had nothing to look forward to for the rest of their lives but prison bars. All in all, it had been a job well done, and now this was Middle Island once more and ahead was Delta.

Dan Scoville was eager to see many people again. Tod Neely, for instance, for the kid had crept deeply into his affections. Then there were Molly Profitt and Bill Profitt and Ed Jethro, friends it would be good to look at and speak to once more. And there was Cole Logan, a man foursquare, despite his mistaken ideas in the past. And finally, out in that sleepy, summer-misted distance ahead, there was a girl—a girl with wonderful gray eyes and a clean, cool beauty which, once discovered, could not be forgotten. . . .

Tod Neely was waiting on the porch in front of the office and he swarmed all over Scoville and was chesty with boyish pride at Scoville's praise at the way the office and inner room had been kept clean and orderly.

Scoville met and talked with Molly and Bill Profitt and with grinning little Ed Jethro. He even went over and saw Mrs. Tyce at her eating house, bringing with him such a cool breeze of refreshing cheerfulness and honest concern that the weary lines in that good woman's face smoothed out somewhat, and she smiled after him when he had gone, and then paused before a small mirror to tidy up her hair a bit.

Back at his office, Scoville sucked on his pipe and fought at the restlessness which nagged him. Suppose he did ride out to the Block L—what excuse could he cook up for the visit? Concern over Cole's wounded leg wouldn't do, for by this time Cole would be as sound as a dollar again. And, bound to be looming at the Logans' always, were the facts around Rack Logan's death.

Any way a man approached that, and no matter how you buttered it up with the best of reasons, the one solid fact remained. He, Dan Scoville, had killed Rack Logan. It did no good to say that Rack was a venomous renegade. Blood was thicker than water and thicker than the edicts of law, too, no matter how well justified an act in behalf of that law might be.

Oh, Cole understood, all right. Cole had been there, been part of those short and ugly moments out there in the swamp at Mudbank. Cole had seen it all, lived his part of it, and knew the stark necessity of the shot that had killed Rack. But how would the rest of the Logans feel? How, in particular, would Loren feel . . . ? Musing these things, Dan Scoville prowled his office with caged restlessness.

Molly Profitt came in, threw him a keen glance, and smiled softly to herself.

"I thought you'd be off riding by this time, Dan Scoville. I'd have thought you'd be eager to see some of your other friends besides those in town."

He squirmed a little. "No rush. Plenty of time."

"No," she corrected, "there isn't plenty of time. Youth always makes that mistake. And I'll bet she's been counting the days, the same as you."

"She?" blurted Scoville. "I don't know what you mean."

Molly Profitt's smile became a gentle laugh. "Shame on you, thinking you can fool me. For there's only one thing that could have brought you back to Delta so full of enthusiasm and bounce. You remind me of a teen-year-old, going to his first dance. All slicked up, but afraid to start."

He looked at her soberly. "There's one fact that nobody can get around, Mrs. Profitt. I killed Rack Logan."

"So you did." She studied him gravely. "The world, being the kind of world it is, makes such things necessary at times. The main thing is—has it left any permanent scar on you? I don't believe it has. As for Rack, if you hadn't taken care of him, then he would certainly have killed you, and probably Cole, too. Oh, I had the whole story from Cole. And he certainly doesn't hold it against you."

"Cole's got a man's viewpoint," Scoville pointed out. "Besides being hardheaded and practical. Women don't reason that way."

"Now don't they!" said Molly Profitt tartly. "You feel that you're an authority on the way a woman's mind and heart work?"

Scoville began to flounder a little. "Well, not exactly. I—but—"

Molly Profitt dropped a hand on his arm, and her smile went soft and gentle again. "Poor man! That wasn't a fair question, was it? Well, I know how a woman's mind and heart work, Dan. I should, being one of those strange and unpredictable creatures. Let me tell you this, boy. In many ways a woman is far more practical and realistic than a man. Particularly in affairs of the heart."

He grinned at her. "Taking a lot for granted, aren't we? By this time she's probably forgotten I'm alive."

"Bosh!" sniffed Molly Profitt. "All her life Loren Logan had lived in a restricted, not entirely natural world. Then you, Dan Scoville, exploded across that world, knocking down barriers, opening doors which led to a freedom of thought and action she'd never known before. Do you think she'd ever forget the man who did that? I don't."

She turned to the door, then paused there. "About Tod Neely, Dan. That youngster has crept very deeply into my heart. You mustn't ever take him completely away from me."

Scoville walked over and put an arm about Molly Profitt's matronly shoulders. "If Tod has crawled into your heart, I know that you've won him completely. In you, Tod sees what he's always yearned for and never really known—a mother. You can have all of Tod that he wants to give, and I know that will be a lot. I'll stand around at the fringe of things, where I belong."

A single tear squeezed its way into being and rolled down Molly Profitt's cheek. At that moment there lifted the soft mutter of hoofs in the street's dust, and heading in, jogging side by side, rode Nora Baine and Loren Logan. Molly Profitt dabbed swiftly at that vagrant tear.

"Heavens alive!" she exclaimed. "She'll think us both utterly shameless if she saw me standing here with your arm around me." She tipped Scoville that gentle, kindly smile. "Thanks, Dan."

She hurried out and turned into the store.

From well back in the shadow of the office, Scoville watched the two girls cut in at an angle toward the store end of the porch. Then, after they'd passed the limit of his vision, he listened intently and heard them move across the porch and go into the store. Through that thin inner wall he heard the light, quick murmur of their voices, heard Bill Profitt's deeper tones.

He moved quietly back and forth across the office, trying to decide what to do. After all, sooner or later, he'd have to find out just how Loren Logan felt toward him—find out if that affair with Rack had left any lasting impression on her. The time might just as well be now. He would, he decided, saunter into the store casually and appear mightily surprised at finding her there. Yeah, that was the way to do it.

He got no chance to put his strategy into effect. For there was a quick step at the door of his office, and then it was Loren Logan herself who stood there.

All that he had remembered about her was there. The same slender grace, the startling beauty, and above all—those clear gray eyes, now softly shining.

"Dan!" she exclaimed. "Dan Scoville! It took you a long time to come back to us."

His spirits leaped, but he held his manner to soberness as he moved a little toward her.

"I don't suppose any excuse will ever wipe out the lasting fact, Loren. It—it was one of those things."

Her eyes widened, showed puzzlement. "I—I don't know what you're talking about, Dan."

"About Rack," plunged Scoville desperately. "In a situation like that one was, a man really hasn't time to think. He just acts instinctively, and fast. That's the way of it, if he wants to stay alive. Rack was throwing his gun and I—well—!" He finished with a shrug.

She seemed almost letdown, some of the shine in her eyes fading. "Oh—that! Cole told me all about it. He said you did only what you had to do—and that you did right. So, it's over and done with, Dan. And forgotten."

"And you don't hold it against me—you don't?"

"Of course not. Why should I?"

He sighed deeply and his voice went a little husky. "I had to get that question about Rack out of the way, Loren. Now—now I want to talk about you—and me?"

Somehow he had both her hands in his. The soft color beat in her throat and cheeks, and her glance, at first a little shy, met and held his steadily and without wavering, and in her eyes there began and grew a deep and wonderful shining.

"About you—and me, Dan," she murmured. "That—that is why I am here—!"

Center Point Large Print
600 Brooks Road / PO Box 1
Thorndike, ME 04986-0001 USA

(207) 568-3717

US & Canada:
1 800 929-9108
www.centerpointlargeprint.com